A FUTURE IN THE BAY

CHASING TIDES BOOK EIGHT

FIONA BAKER

JOIN MY NEWSLETTER

If you love beachy, feel-good women's fiction, sign up to receive my newsletter, where you'll get free books, exclusive bonus content, and info on my new releases and sales!

CHAPTER ONE

Dr. Gwen Dunaway frowned a little as she drove her car along the streets of Blueberry Bay. The small Rhode Island town was charming, she couldn't deny it, but she wasn't paying too much attention to it. She was concentrating on locating the building that she'd bought to be her new private medical practice.

She scolded herself for buying it sight-unseen—if she'd at least taken a tour of it first, she would know where it was located. But she'd been so busy getting everything in order, trying to sell her practice in New Hampshire as soon as possible.

Her shoulders tightened a little as she thought about the life she'd left behind in New Hampshire. The truth was that she could have taken more time to move herself to an entirely new place, but she'd wanted to move as soon as possible. She was a successful doctor, and her practice had been going well—but her life at home hadn't been.

She tucked a strand of her bobbed brown hair behind her ear and tried to concentrate on the road. Despite her efforts, into her mind floated a memory of her long-term boyfriend Ron, standing in the doorway of her kitchen and telling her that he didn't think things between them were going to work anymore. She pressed her lips together as she remembered his words.

"You're too inflexible, Gwen. It's like nothing matters more to you than things being done the right way."

She shook her head as she made a turn in the road, following the prompting of her GPS.

I'm not too inflexible, she thought firmly. *I'm a successful woman who focuses on her career. He used to say that was just fine with him. Successful people need to be careful about details in order to stay on top of their goals.*

She swallowed, feeling a heaviness in her chest. The truth was that she hadn't felt in love with Ron for a long time, but he'd been her partner and New Hampshire had been her home. Now she found herself completely starting over at the age of thirty-six—something that she'd never seen coming.

"You've arrived," announced the robotic voice of her GPS. Gwen slowed her car down in front of the small red brick building and frowned.

"This can't be it," she muttered.

It was much too small, and much too unassuming. There were a couple of small trees planted along the sidewalk in front of it—trees that would practically make it invisible when they grew to full height. The buildings on either side of it were brightly colored—a pink hair salon and a white stone clothing store that had aqua blue shutters. By comparison, the little building that she'd purchased seemed to be practically invisible.

And it was so small—or at least it appeared to be from the outside. She told herself that couldn't be it, and there must be some mistake. She could have sworn that the place she'd looked at online was much bigger than that. The pictures she'd seen online had been of a place that looked sleek and professional, and amply sized. This place looked like it could fit inside a shoebox.

She admitted to herself with a grimace that it was possible she'd been in such a rush to move out of

New Hampshire and move on that she hadn't paid too much attention to the pictures.

"There must be some mistake," she muttered again, and pulled her car into the parking spot in front of the building. She turned off the engine of her car and picked up her phone, checking the address. The one she'd typed into her GPS matched the building she was staring at. Even so, she told herself that maybe the addresses had gotten mixed up, and there was a mistake. She texted her nurse Heidi Rhodes, who was arriving in Blueberry Bay the next day and had helped her pick out the building.

GWEN: Hey, I think I might have gone to the wrong place. Is this the building we bought?

She sent along a photograph of the place along with her text, keeping her fingers crossed that Heidi was about to reply and assure her that she'd definitely gone to the wrong location.

For a few minutes, she sat in the car, waiting for a reply and blinking doubtfully at the small red brick building. Even though it was a chilly spring day, the sidewalks were busy with people walking along them. She saw kids running ahead of their parents, teenagers walking along giggling and holding cups of coffee, and people walking a variety of adorable dogs.

She smiled quietly to herself. Whatever else happened, she seemed to have picked a good place to start over in. Blueberry Bay seemed charming and full of life, and she'd always wanted to live right by the ocean. She told herself that things were going to get better for her, just as soon as she got back onto her own two feet.

She turned to look back at the building, wincing a little bit. Maybe it was just her nerves being rattled by uprooting herself and going somewhere new, but she felt that the place was entirely unsatisfactory. She bit her lip, regretting the fact that she hadn't gone to check out the place in person before purchasing it.

Her phone buzzed with a text message, and her heart leapt up, hoping that Heidi would tell her that she'd gone to the wrong place.

HEIDI: Hey! Nope, that's the right spot. Cute, isn't it?

Gwen let out a long sigh, deciding that Heidi was entirely too optimistic. She gave the building another long stare, this time trying to reconcile herself to the fact that it was definitely hers. She'd purchased it, and there was no going back on everything now.

"At least it's better than staying in New Hampshire," she muttered.

In addition to being the location of her private medical practice, the red brick building also doubled as her new home. There was an apartment upstairs, and she turned her eyes to the upper windows of the building curiously. It looked like an old place. She hoped it hadn't fallen into too much disrepair. She didn't want a place with creaky floorboards and moldy cupboards.

Sighing again, she climbed out of her car and walked around to the trunk, where her suitcase was. She tugged it out, grunting a little. She was of medium height, but frequent running had made her fit, so even a massive, heavy suitcase wasn't too much for her to manage.

Once she had it placed on the sidewalk, she closed the trunk of her car and locked it. She looked up and noticed that a couple of passing pedestrians were eyeing her curiously—but in a friendly way, with smiles. They looked almost as if they were hoping to introduce themselves. She smiled back, but she didn't feel in the mood to make friends just then. She wanted to get inside the building and see if the inside was any less disappointing than the outside.

The pedestrians passed by, and she began to roll

her suitcase toward the front door of the clinic. She lugged it through the front door, closing her eyes as she went. She took a few steps into the main room and then opened her eyes.

It wasn't terrible. It was functional, certainly. It had a front desk and beyond that she could see an examination room. Leaving her suitcase in the lobby area, she walked past the desk into the examination room and flipped on the light.

She nodded slowly as she looked around the room. It was functional, definitely, but far from fancy. The walls were painted an off-white which had seen cleaner days, and she made a mental note to repaint the walls as soon as possible. Probably tomorrow. It shouldn't take too long. The equipment all appeared to be in good working order, and ultimately, that was all that really mattered.

It will have to do, she thought, sighing again. *At least the inside is better than the outside—and I can doctor up the inside pretty easily.*

She smiled wryly at her unintentional pun, taking one more look around the examination room. She stepped out of it and began to explore the rest of the clinic—looking into closets and bathrooms and taking mental notes on what they needed to stock up on.

Once she'd finished exploring, she stood again in the lobby, watching the sunlight flicker across the floorboards. Unexpectedly, she felt a moment of peace and relief, and a surge of gratitude that she had the chance to start a new life.

Things were going to get better, she told herself firmly. She might have started out her time in Blueberry Bay with a disappointment, but that meant that things could only go up from there.

She picked up her suitcase and began to roll it toward a doorway that was marked "Private, Do Not Enter." She smiled to herself as she opened it—there was something fun about owning the secret space behind a "forbidden" door.

In front of her was a narrow staircase, and she grimaced, realizing how difficult it was going to be to lug her giant suitcase up it. She took a deep breath and squared her shoulders, and then started up the steps, tugging her suitcase along behind her.

By the time she reached the upper apartment, she was out of breath and sweating along her hairline. She pushed open the upper door with her shoulder and stepped inside her new apartment.

It was very cute, she couldn't deny it. It was also definitely old—she could tell from the windows and the arched doorways—but it had been excellently maintained, and she found it charming. Leaving her suitcase by the front door, she started to explore it with interest, scampering from room to room almost girlishly.

As she explored, she pictured where all of her things were going to go. The rest of her belongings were arriving the next day, and she felt excited about beginning to nestle into her new home. It was just the right size—large enough to feel roomy, and small enough to be cozy. She pictured where she wanted to put her couch, and where she wanted to hang various framed prints she still had.

If I squint hard enough, I can picture this place filled with my own things, she thought, feeling impatient to make it feel less empty.

She realized that she should go back downstairs and lock the front door—she was used to never leaving anything unlocked back at her former place. Her stomach grumbled, and she reminded herself that she would need to get dinner for herself at some point. She would probably order takeout. She felt too tired to try to cook something—and then she realized she was silly to even consider it, since her pots and pans were still in boxes inside the moving van.

Suddenly feeling exhausted, she went back down the narrow staircase. It was almost surprising how quick of a trip it was, in comparison to how long it had taken her to bring the suitcase upstairs.

She crossed the small lobby in a few short strides and locked the front door. Outside the windows of her practice, she could see that dusk was beginning to fall. She realized that her apartment was going to be mostly dark before her lamps arrived.

She sat down on one of the chairs in the lobby. It was as if all of the feelings that she'd been rushing around trying to avoid feeling caught up with her in that moment.

She looked around at the little lobby and sighed, thinking about the blur that had been her last few weeks. Suddenly she missed her old life terribly—she didn't feel ready for everything to change like this, all at once. She'd wanted to escape New Hampshire and get a fresh start.

But was this really the right answer?

Isaiah Dunlap grinned to himself as he parked his motorcycle on the street outside Blueberry Bay's Little Clams Elementary School. He was there to surprise his sister Olivia Dunlap, who was a teacher at the school. She didn't expect him to arrive until the next day, and he was gleefully making his way inside the school unbeknownst to her.

He pulled his phone out of his pocket and double-checked his last text from Olivia, stating that she was getting work done at the school that afternoon. He glanced at the time, making sure she was still inside the building, and grinned.

He'd always been one for surprises. And pranks. He'd pulled some truly impressive pranks on Olivia when they were growing up—but today's surprise was sure to make her happy. The plastic frogs in her cereal when she was eight hadn't made her too happy.

He got off his motorcycle, already feeling stealthy, even though he'd been sneaky enough to ask her to send him a picture of her classroom, so he knew that the windows faced the opposite street. He walked toward the back entrance of the school, trying to look casual, with his hands tucked into the pockets of his leather jacket.

He knew from Olivia that classes were over for the day, but there were still a fair amount of cars parked in the parking lot of Little Clams. He figured that other teachers were doing what Olivia was doing—choosing to get work done there at the school instead of at home. Maybe there was even a meeting or something going on.

He began to whistle as he strolled up to the back door, and then he stopped himself. He shouldn't be whistling—that might draw attention to himself. Olivia might be anywhere around the school instead of in her classroom—he didn't want her to glance out a window and see him.

He rang the buzzer of the back door and was let inside. He stopped by the office to check in, and the receptionist gave him a conspiratorial grin when he said he was there to surprise his sister Olivia.

"Do you know where her classroom is?" the receptionist asked.

"Not exactly—could you point me in the right direction?" He flashed a charismatic grin, and she grinned back.

"Down the hall, to the left, and then four doors down. Her name will be on the door so you can't miss it."

"Perfect. Thanks for your help!"

He stepped back out into the hallway, repressing an urge to whistle again. He felt excited to see his sister—it had been way too long since he'd been able to spend time with her. He was eager to have some quality time with her in Blueberry Bay.

As he passed one of the playrooms, his eyes lighted on a Jack-in-the-Box that was resting on one of the little tables.

"Oh, that will be perfect," he muttered, and stepped inside the room to borrow the toy.

He went back to walking stealthily as soon as he was in the hallway that her classroom was in. He could see the door to her classroom left ajar, and for a moment his heart flopped in disappointment, wondering if she'd gone home already. Then he heard the sound of her favorite 1990's girl band playing from inside the classroom, along with the sound of her singing along to the album. Grinning, he poked his head around the doorway and saw her standing in the far corner of the room, organizing art supplies on a long table.

He guessed that she was preparing for the next day's class, and she seemed to be engrossed in her work. Almost silently, he tiptoed inside the classroom. She didn't notice, and he suppressed a grin of triumph. He wound up the Jack-in-the-Box that he was carrying, set it on one of the desks, and then darted to hide behind the open door.

He only had to wait a few seconds before the Jack-in-the-Box popped open and Olivia yelled with surprise, whirling and dropping the box of colored pencils that she was holding.

"What on earth?" she cried.

"Surprise!" he yelled, popping out from behind the door.

Olivia let out a squeal and raced into his arms. "What are you doing here?" she gushed, rocking him back and forth. "I thought you weren't getting here until tomorrow."

"What part of surprise don't you understand?" he teased, grinning at her.

"You scamp!" She swatted him in the arm. "You're more of a child than any of the kids at school!" Despite her scolding, it was clear from the way that her eyes were shining that she was thrilled to see him—and she wasn't too upset about the prank.

He bowed dramatically, still grinning. "I thought you liked Jack-in-the-Boxes."

"Sure, when I know they're about to go off!"

"But you're happy to see me, right?"

She grinned at him. "I'm so happy to see you. I can't deny it. I know you're going to be here for a couple of months, but the extra day still feels like a huge bonus."

"Complete with jump scare and a brother. What more could you possibly want?"

She wrinkled her nose at him. "How about just the brother?"

"It's too late for that."

"Okay, but no more jump scares."

He grinned mischievously.

"Isaiah! I mean it. Look me in the eyes. No more jump scares."

He sighed. "Fine. I promise, no more jump scares for the remainder of the visit."

"Good. Thank you."

"Thank you," he said, privately noting that she hadn't said anything about pranks and feeling gleeful. "Do you need any help setting up that art table over there?"

"Yeah, if you want! We can both get out of here faster that way."

They went over to the art table, and she instructed him to put a tube of washable glue at every place.

"How's North Carolina?" she asked as she organized colored sheets of paper into stacks containing green, blue, and yellow.

"Great as ever," he said, smiling at her. "You should see what they did to the town hall. There's a massive mural on the side of it now—it's really nice-looking."

"You should have sent me pictures!"

"Google can show you." He laughed.

She paused in her work to look up pictures of their hometown's town hall and cooed over how nice it looked.

"Oh, I love that. Any more updates from home? Anybody get married or have a baby?"

For the next few minutes, Isaiah caught his sister up on everything that had happened in the place where they'd grown up together. She listened eagerly —he knew she still had a lot of affection for their hometown even though she'd moved away a few years earlier.

He hadn't told her yet, but he was also looking to move somewhere new. He felt like he needed a change of scenery, and he was feeling the tug to live somewhere else. When she'd asked him if he'd be willing to come to Blueberry Bay for a couple of months to help her with a project, he'd agreed immediately. He was happy to go somewhere new for a while—at the very least, it would scratch the itch he'd been feeling to relocate, and at best, it would help him decide where he wanted to move to. Blueberry Bay was a cozy town right by the water—

living there could give him a sense of whether or not he wanted to live in a place like that, or somewhere completely different, like a bustling city.

"How are things here?" he asked, coming to help her with organizing the stacks of paper since he'd finished with the glue sticks. "How's that heartthrob you're in love with?"

She laughed and blushed. She was dating Corey Easton, a local souvenir shop owner with two rambunctious twins that Olivia adored. "He's doing great. Max and Haley are doing great, and the store is going great."

"And you're great, so the man is really lucky." He grinned. "I'm excited to meet him and the kids."

"I'm so excited for you to meet them! You're going to love them, I know you are."

"How about the rest of your life? How's teaching?"

"Going so well. You know how much I love kids, and the classes here have been fun and just the right amount of work, you know? It never feels like too much."

He smiled at his sister, wondering if what she considered to be the perfect amount of work might feel like too much to some other people—enthusiastic people were like that about what they had to do.

"I'm glad to hear that. Speaking of work, before we leave the school today, you should show me all the places you want to renovate."

"Sure! I want shelves put into some of the classrooms, and some equipment added to the playground. Some other things too, here and there." She frowned a little, pressing her lips together. "The school board has approved everything that I proposed, but they want the work done before Kids' Fest in mid-April. That doesn't give you a lot of time."

He grinned at her. "We'll get it done! And besides, I'm sure the school board is happy with you for proposing improvements and offering to accomplish them through very cheap labor via your brother."

She winced. "They are paying you, you know—I know it's probably not as much as it should be—"

He laughed, shaking his head. "I'm happy to do it. It's for a good cause, and what they're paying will more than cover my expenses. Especially if my loving sister feeds me dinner sometimes."

She laughed. "You got it. You can always come over to my place for dinner—sometimes Corey and the kids come over or I go over there, but it would be easy to add you onto the dinner guest list." Raising her brows, she added, "Speaking of places to eat food, where did you end up staying? Are you at Literary Stays?"

He shook his head. "No, I've got a furnished apartment by the water. It's a short-term lease, just for the amount of time I need to be here working on the renovations."

"Sounds great! I'll have to swing by sometime soon to see it. Is it cute?"

He laughed. "If by 'cute,' you mean small, then yes. I like it. It's got a little balcony overlooking the ocean, and a kitchen, and an itty-bitty bedroom. And there's a garage underneath where I can keep my baby."

She grinned, knowing that he was referring to his motorcycle. "You know, for a guy who looks so tough and rough-around-the-edges, you have a kind of peculiar nickname for your motorcycle."

He shrugged, grinning. "All the tough bikers call their motorcycle their baby. You can ask anybody."

"Well, you're the only tough biker I know, so I'll have to take your word for it."

They finished setting up the craft supplies, and then she took him on a tour of the school, showing him all the places where she wanted him to make renovations.

"Is it too much?" she asked nervously as they were circling back from the playground. "Do you think you'll be able to finish it by mid-April?"

"For sure," he assured her, grinning confidently. "I'll get started tomorrow, bright and early in the morning. Next time you show up here, you're going to be like, 'Wow, he's done already.'"

She laughed. "Oh, am I now?"

"Definitely."

Chuckling, they went back inside the school together, since it was still early spring and chilly. When they were back in Olivia's classroom, they sat down across from each other at a couple of desks.

"You know what else your school needs?" he joked. "Bigger desks. I can barely fit in this thing."

She laughed, shaking her head. "What are your plans after this?"

"I want to go see Aunt Marsha. I haven't seen her since she and Willis started dating, and I want to hear all about how she's doing. And I want to meet Willis."

His sister's eyes lit up at the mention of their favorite aunt, Marsha Dunlap, and her boyfriend Willis Jenkins. He knew that Olivia had had a hand in bringing the two of them together, since they'd been in love many years earlier and had both been skittish about starting to date again after so long a time.

"I've heard so much about him, I'm really looking forward to meeting him," he said.

"So you can formally offer your approval?" she teased.

"Hey, anyone that makes Aunt Marsha that happy already has my approval. And the same goes for Corey," he added warmly.

She tucked her hair behind her ear, blushing a little. "Well, I can't wait to hear about how meeting Willis goes, and I can't wait for you to meet Corey and the kids."

They stood up and gave each other a hug.

"I'll see you soon, sis," he said, playfully punching her shoulder.

"You'd better!" She grinned at him and waved as he left the classroom.

When he was back in the hallway, he put his hands into his pockets and began to whistle freely.

I really like Blueberry Bay already, he thought cheerfully. *It's going to be a great couple of months.*

CHAPTER TWO

Caitlin frowned down at the magazine clippings that were spread out around her on the living room rug. Beautiful images of centerpieces and table settings and flower arrangements surrounded her, but instead of smiling at them, she was biting her lip.

When she and Michael had decided to change their wedding from a simple courthouse ceremony to a big, elaborate celebration on the beach, she'd been nothing but excited at first, even though she'd known how much work it was going to be. Now she was starting to feel stressed and overwhelmed by the whole process—their wedding was fast approaching, and the decisions seemed to be never-ending. She was already a busy woman, since she owned a dinner cruise and had a daughter to raise. Planning a whole wedding in a short amount of time had added a great deal to her workload, even though her fiancé, Michael, was also doing the planning with her.

Pearl, her eight-year-old daughter, scampered up behind her and gave her a hug.

"What are you doing?" she asked curiously, looking down at the pictures with her curly head close to her mother's. "Planning the wedding?"

"I am," Caitlin said with a sigh. She mustered a smile. "You want to help me?"

"I would love to!" Pearl sat down on the carpet next to Caitlin without hesitation. "All of these look so pretty."

Caitlin beamed at her, feeling glad that Pearl's enthusiasm had been added to the task at hand. "What about this one?" she asked, handing Pearl a picture of twinkling lights bordering a dinner table.

"Ooh, I love that!" Pearl cooed. "And it will look even better at your wedding, because your wedding will be on the beach. And the dinner will happen at night, so all the lights will be reflecting on the water too, and then there will be sparkles everywhere."

Caitlin smiled, feeling a new rush of enthusiasm. "You're right," she said. "That's a really lovely point, Pearl."

"I know," Pearl said cheerfully, and picked up

another one of the drawings. "Oh, this one is so pretty! If you put candles on every table like that, your wedding will look like fairyland."

Caitlin couldn't help but get a warm feeling in her chest. She felt grateful that she got to have that moment with her daughter, and that Pearl was going to be part of a big celebration of her and Michael's love.

"I agree." She glanced down at her daughter. "What do you think we should pick for candles? Tall ones like these, or little tea lights?"

Pearl pressed her lips together in concentration for a moment, and then reached for another picture. "Do this," she said. "The tall candles but with three different heights. That will help with the sparkle effect."

"Good idea." Caitlin grinned and picked up the picture, adding it to her pile of ideas she wanted to use. "Do you think we should use white candles or colored candles?"

"Hmm." Pearl looked down at the rest of the photographs, inspecting them carefully. Caitlin found the little girl's frown of concentration endearing. "I like white better."

"Me too. And white candles will be cheaper too."

"That's good. Weddings are expensive."

Caitlin hid a smile, amused by the way Pearl seemed to be parroting what she'd heard the adults say. She watched her daughter with affection for a moment, feeling a rush of gratitude for Pearl's optimistic spirit. After Caitlin's divorce from Pearl's father, the two of them had moved to Blueberry Bay, and the little girl's attitude had always been stellar. Despite all of the upheaval in their lives, Pearl had remained resilient.

I'm so glad we're having this big celebration, Caitlin thought, still watching her daughter. *Not only does Michael deserve it, but Pearl does too.*

She saw how excited Pearl was about the upcoming wedding, and she reflected that celebrating her and Michael's marriage with a big ceremony and reception would help Pearl with the new life transition they were about to make. Pearl already adored Michael and saw him as a father figure in her life, but Caitlin felt that a wedding celebration was the right way to honor the fact that their little family was becoming official. It would make it all seem more real and exciting to Pearl, more of a big deal than going to the courthouse.

"How many more days until the end of April?"

Pearl asked, turning to her mother with an impatient grin.

"Not enough." Caitlin laughed. "We still have too much to do!"

Pearl patted her mother's shoulder reassuringly. "It's going to be okay, Mom. We'll get it done together. I'll help you."

Caitlin grinned at her daughter. "Thanks, honey. That makes me feel better about everything."

"What else do we need to decide on?"

"Well, tablecloths. We need to decide if we want crushed satin, or plain satin, or this embroidered sheer overlay—"

"Oh, pick that one!" Pearl said, clapping her hands. She pointed to the sheer overlay. "That one with all the roses embroidered into it."

"You're right, it is really pretty, isn't it?"

For the next half an hour, Caitlin and Pearl continued to look at the wedding pictures, making all kinds of important decisions about decorations. None of the decisions were final—Caitlin wanted to run everything by Michael first—but she felt great about what they picked out. It was fun to spend time with Pearl and get her opinions on things—Pearl's choices were always for the prettiest options, and

Caitlin found that she agreed with her daughter most of the time.

"There's one more thing we need to pick out," she said as they were organizing the remaining pictures into a discard pile.

"What's that? The rings?"

"No, Michael and I already picked out the rings," Caitlin said, thinking about the rings that they had chosen together with a rush of excitement. Both rings were elegant, and hers was studded with small pearls, beautiful reminders of her daughter and the oceanside town where they lived. "What we need to pick out right now is something else. Something very important." She stood up and went to get her laptop from where it was resting on the dining room table.

"What?" the little girl asked eagerly, turning around on the carpet.

"Your flower girl dress," Caitlin answered, and Pearl clapped her hands with excitement.

Caitlin sat back down next to her daughter, opening her laptop. "We can look for dresses online," she said. "That way we have the widest variety of options to choose from."

"Oh, I can't wait," Pearl said as Caitlin started to search for dresses. "Can it be pink?"

Caitlin chuckled. "It can absolutely be pink. The

bridesmaids are going to be in a sea blue, so that will go nicely with pink. You'll look like a pink flower at the edge of the ocean." She winked, and Pearl grinned.

They didn't have to look long before Pearl gasped at the sight of one of the little dresses. "Oh, that's it!" she exclaimed, leaning forward and peering at the screen. "That one's perfect." She was gazing at a pink, frilly dress with a full skirt. "It looks like a princess dress."

"I agree," Caitlin said, also finding the dress absolutely charming. "You'll look adorable in that, Pearl."

"Thank you, Mom!" Pearl hugged Caitlin tightly. "I love it!"

At that moment, they heard the back door open, and Pearl let out a squeal of excitement.

"Michael!"

The little girl scampered off to meet him, and Caitlin stood more slowly, smiling to herself as she set her laptop down on the dining room table.

Michael and Pearl appeared a moment later—the little girl was dragging him along by the hand, intent on showing him the dress that she and Caitlin had just picked out.

"Look what we found!" she said, leading him up

to the laptop and gesturing to the picture. "That's going to be my flower girl dress."

Michael shared a quick grin with Caitlin before giving his full attention to the dress. He leaned forward and looked at the dress with a genuine smile of excitement. "Pearl, that's so pretty! Good choice."

He fist-bumped the little girl, who giggled happily.

"Now we need to show you everything else we picked out for the wedding," Pearl said. "You're going to love all of it."

She skipped over to the pile of pictures that she and Caitlin decided on, bringing it back to the dining room table. Michael turned to Caitlin with shining eyes.

"You two were picking stuff out?"

"We'll only go with these if you also like them," Caitlin said, wrapping her arms around him and giving him a quick kiss. "Pearl had some great suggestions."

"Yes, I did," Pearl said proudly, starting to lay the pictures out across the table.

Michael and Caitlin shared another grin, and then Michael leaned forward to look at the pictures.

"Oh, these look fantastic," he said.

"You like the white candles?" Caitlin asked,

keeping her arm linked through his. "We were thinking those would look more elegant than pink or blue ones, alongside everything else we picked out."

"And they're cheaper," Pearl said importantly.

"Absolutely." Michael's eyes shone with excitement. "Do you think we could add seashells to the centerpieces?"

"Oh, that's a great idea!" Caitlin and Pearl both exclaimed at the same time, and then all three of them started laughing.

"Glad you approve," Michael teased.

They finished showing him the rest of the pictures, and he loved all their ideas.

"You're both geniuses," he said, kissing Pearl's head. "This is going to be the most beautiful wedding there ever was." He turned to Caitlin with shining eyes, and she had a feeling he was thinking what she was thinking—that to them, it really was going to be the most beautiful wedding because they got to marry each other.

She grinned at Michael, feeling a rush of happiness. It didn't matter how much work she needed to do first—she was counting down the days until this man became her husband.

* * *

Mid-afternoon sunlight streamed across Alissa Taylor's desk as she typed with adept fingers at her laptop. She was smiling quietly to herself as she worked, since the topic of the article she was writing was something that made her happy.

"What do you think of this?" she called to Josie Cliff, *The Outlet*'s secretary, and her husband, Dane Taylor. She read aloud from her draft, "One of Blueberry Bay's most dedicated teachers, Olivia Dunlap, has proved just how much she cares about Little Clams Elementary School by arranging for renovations to be made to the school before the springtime Kids' Fest celebration."

"Sounds great to me," Josie said, taking a sip of her coffee. A beautiful wedding ring sparkled on her hand, and she grinned affectionately at Alissa. She had seemed to glow with more happiness than usual ever since her marriage to Wesley.

"Good, but can you add something about her brother right away in the first sentence?" Dane called from inside his office. "That's the best angle of the story."

"You got it, boss!" she called back cheerfully, pushing her glasses up on her nose.

Taking a sip of her lavender latte—Dane had gone out and brought them all back beverages from

Tidal Wave Coffee earlier—she narrowed her eyes at her computer in concentration. She set her coffee cup down and continued to type, editing her first sentence and then expanding the article.

She wrote about Olivia, finding it fun to write an article about one of her good friends. She described how Olivia was spearheading the renovations for the elementary school and going above and beyond to get it all done. She smiled as she worked, reflecting that this was one of her favorite articles she'd ever composed. She was very fond of Olivia, and she liked the idea of renovations being made to the school—a school that her and Dane's baby Oscar would go to when he was old enough. She glanced down at her pregnant belly for a moment, feeling a glow of anticipation.

After she'd been writing for a while, a notification popped up on her phone.

"Hey, sweetheart!" she called to Dane. "The crib is being delivered soon! I should go." She finished her coffee quickly and stood up, beginning to pack up her laptop.

Dane poked his head out of his office. "Are you sure you don't want me to go?"

"I won't try to lift the box, I promise." She laughed. "But one of us has so sign for it, and you're busier than me today. Besides, I can finish up my articles at home. I'll make sure to finish that 'How to Babyproof Your Home' article for the homeowner's column."

Recently in their magazine's homeowner's column, in which they highlighted useful tips for home repair, they'd been focusing on things having to do with babyproofing specifically. She'd enjoyed it immensely—and found it easy to do, since they were spending a great deal of time learning how to babyproof their own home.

"That's okay, sweetheart, you don't have to do it today," he said, giving her the concerned look she'd grown so used to. Ever since she'd gotten pregnant, he'd been watching over her like a hawk. "You can do it tomorrow."

She waved her hand through the air as if to wave his words away, smiling at him. "I'll do it today—I'm enjoying writing it."

"Well, okay, but promise me you'll take it easy."

She walked across the office with her laptop bag slung over her shoulder and gave him a kiss. "I will."

She said goodbye to Dane and Josie and stepped outside into the spring afternoon. It was warmer that day than it had been the day before, and she took a deep breath of the air, enjoying the way it smelled of things beginning to grow.

She got into her car and drove back to their house in a few short minutes. She was just in time to catch the delivery man and sign for the package, which he offered to bring into the front entryway of the house for her.

Once that was all settled and the delivery man had driven off, she sat down at the kitchen table with her laptop, getting ready to resume her work on the babyproofing article.

Her fingers moved at a regular speed at first, but after a few minutes, her mind started to slow down with sleepiness. The sunlight flickering across the kitchen table was warm and soothing, and she found herself being lulled into a heavy, pleasant drowsiness.

The next thing she knew, she was snapping awake to the sound of someone knocking on the front door.

"Oh," she grunted, stretching and looking at the time. She'd only dozed off for a few minutes, but her neck felt stiff from sleeping sitting up. "Coming!" she called after whoever was at the front door knocked again.

She hurried to the front door and opened it, and her face broke into a grin when she saw that it was her mother-in-law, Johanna Taylor, standing there. She was surprised to see her, but very glad to. Johanna's brown hair was pulled back into a tidy chignon, and she was wearing a beautiful purple sweater that Alissa guessed her friend, Marsha Dunlap, had knitted for her.

"Hey, Johanna!" she said, giving the older woman a hug. "To what do I owe the surprise?"

"I brought over a casserole for you two for dinner," Johanna said, smiling warmly. "It's filled with all kinds of good things—noodles and tomatoes and black olives. It's an old family recipe. Dane loves it."

"Oh! That's so thoughtful of you. I didn't expect anyone to bring us meals until after the baby was born." Alissa laughed.

Johanna spoke delicately. "Well, Dane told me that you've been a bit tired lately. I thought I could step in and help you take it easy. Remember you're growing a whole person; you need your rest."

"You're right," Alissa said, glancing down at her growing belly. "I keep thinking I'm all right, that I've got plenty of energy to keep going on, but I was dozing off just now before you got here."

Johanna tutted affectionately, and the two of them went into the kitchen together.

"The casserole is pre-made," Johanna said, turning on the oven, "but it should cook for another hour or so. It's similar to a lasagna."

"That should be perfect—it'll be ready right when Dane will be getting home from the office."

"I know," Johanna said, and Alissa grinned to herself as her mother-in-law placed the casserole dish into the oven. Timing things out carefully was typical of the efficient Johanna—Alissa wasn't surprised that her mother-in-law had arrived with the meal at the right time so that it would be ready by dinnertime.

"Now," Johanna said, straightening and grinning at Alissa. "I think it's time to watch our favorite show."

"Oh! Well, I should—" Alissa glanced at her laptop, and remembered the way she'd just fallen asleep. "I guess I do need to rest." She laughed. "Perfect. Let's go watch our show."

The women trooped into the living room together and settled down comfortably on the couch. Johanna used the remote to find their favorite show, and they settled in to rewatch a season that they'd both already seen. They had bonded over the home renovation show when they'd both had broken bones, and their relationship had been significantly closer ever since.

"Oh, I remember this!" Johanna said eagerly. "This is the cottage with that amazing loft. This is one of my favorite episodes."

"Mine too." Alissa looked over at her mother-in-law, feeling grateful for her. Johanna had proved to be a fun and steadfast companion, and she felt happy that their relationship had deepened and changed as much as it had. All at once, she felt a rush of affection for her mother-in-law, and she leaned over to give her a big hug.

"Thank you," she said. "For the food and for coming over and spending time with me. And reminding me that I need to rest. And for being a good friend."

Johanna flushed a little, smiling warmly and hugging Alissa back tightly. "You're so welcome," she said softly. "Thank you for being a good friend."

The two women smiled affectionately at each other and went back to watching their show. A few minutes later, Johanna got up to make them both cups of peppermint tea.

Alissa sighed with contentment as she sipped the fragrant tea. Her feet were resting on the ottoman, and she was snuggled up with a soft blanket. She hadn't realized how much she needed some rest until she was there getting it.

She glanced over at Johanna again and smiled quietly to herself. The savory aroma of the casserole filled the house while the two women laughed and chatted over their show, waiting for Dane to come home for dinner.

CHAPTER THREE

Gwen looked around the office of her clinic with a sigh of satisfaction. In only a very short amount of time, she'd gotten the place to look far more polished and professional than it had when she'd arrived. She looked out the window, noting that the early morning sky was a cloudless blue. She told herself firmly that today was going to be a good day.

I'm silly to be nervous, she thought, scolding herself. *It's not like it's my first day as a doctor.*

She had to admit, though, she cared very much about their first official day as an open clinic in Blueberry Bay going well. She wanted to ensure that whatever reputation her clinic earned in the town, it was a good one—ideally, a great one. Her practice had been well spoken of in New Hampshire, so she had plenty of reason to be optimistic. No matter how much she told herself that though, it didn't make the butterflies in her stomach go away.

She stepped out of her office into the lobby, which she had also spent time redecorating. She'd replaced the photographs hanging on the walls with canvases of beautiful modern art in pastel colors. She'd also put in new chairs for the waiting area—chairs that were more comfortable and also more modern-looking.

"Big day!" Heidi, Gwen's nurse, walked over to her with a grin. "Are you excited?"

"Yes," Gwen said, even though it was essentially a lie. She wasn't excited—eager, maybe. She felt too nervous about things going right to describe her emotions as excited. "Are we all ready?"

"Oh, definitely. We were all ready yesterday. Everything's sanitized, everything's well-stocked. We're all set." Heidi gave Gwen a cheerful smile, but Gwen could see the young blonde woman's intelligent eyes glittering with sympathetic perception. She had a feeling that Heidi could see straight through her and she knew exactly how nervous she was.

"Great." Gwen returned her smile briskly. "What does our schedule today look like?"

Heidi looked at the clipboard she was carrying. "Our first patient is at two o'clock, and we have seven more after that, scattered throughout the afternoon."

Disappointment flopped in Gwen's stomach. "So few?" she asked, crossing her arms and lifting her shoulders a little. "Is the schedule always going to be this empty, I wonder?"

"I wouldn't worry about it." Heidi hugged her clipboard in a relaxed manner, and Gwen noticed that there were tiny pictures of kittens printed on the fabric of her scrubs. "This is a small town, and you've only just arrived. Once word gets out about your practice, people will come more often. I mean, it's only the first day. Word of mouth hasn't done anything for you yet."

"True." Gwen turned to look out the window onto the sidewalk. People were strolling past, but none of them seemed to be looking at the clinic with any interest. "Maybe we need a bigger sign."

"How about some flowers along the windowsill?" Heidi suggested. "Or a window box? That might draw people's attention to the building."

"That's a great idea. And we could paint the name of the practice on the window," Gwen said, her mind racing with excitement as she had the idea. "In

white letters. Something elegant but big enough to
be noticeable."

"Sounds great to me!" Heidi smiled cheerfully.
She was still only in her mid-twenties, and always
seemed to have energy and enthusiasm.

Gwen smiled at her gratefully, but she still felt
uncertain about everything. Her body seemed to be
humming with restlessness. Painting the name of the
practice in the window and going out to buy flowers
were great ideas, but she couldn't do either of them
at the moment. She could leave the clinic briefly if
she needed to since there were no patients scheduled
for hours, but she didn't want to leave for long or go
very far in case there was a walk-in appointment.

"I'm getting coffee," she announced suddenly.
"What would you like?"

"Oh! Sure! Thanks." Heidi grinned. "How about
a Frappuccino?"

"You got it. I'll be back soon."

"I'll hold down the fort till you get back," Heidi
said, saluting Gwen playfully.

Gwen smiled, glad that at least one of them was
still in high spirits. She grabbed her purse and
stepped out the front door of the clinic into the
spring sunshine. The wind that day was chilly as
usual, but she could feel that the sunlight was

warmer than it had been. There was a fragrance of flowers in the air, and she took some deep breaths as she walked along the sidewalks of Blueberry Bay.

She reached her car, which was parked along the street about halfway down the block. She climbed into it, pulling up her GPS on her phone to look for a coffee shop.

"Oh," she murmured, pleasantly surprised to find that there was one a very short drive away and that it had five stars. "Tidal Wave Coffee, huh?"

She drove to the coffee shop, glad that she could go somewhere close by and not take much time away from the clinic. She felt antsy, and even without patients scheduled for the morning, she wanted to be there. She told herself that she felt that way because they might get a walk-in, but in the back of her mind she knew that she wanted to be there because it felt like the only way to try to control her situation at the moment.

As she drove, she marveled at how small the town was. She turned onto a street that led up to the water, and she could see where the buildings ended and the ocean began. Her previous drives through the town had showed her how small it was in the other directions as well.

All of the shops surrounding her were well cared

for and quaint, and the people walking around seemed to be comfortable in their surroundings. There was a homey, wholesome atmosphere about the place—it was the most "small town" small town that she'd ever been to before.

It seems like a nice place, she thought, glancing at the library as she passed it. *It seems like the people here care about this place a lot.*

But it was so small. What if it was too small for her? What if all of her workdays were like this, with hardly anything to do? She felt she would be unhappy without enough work. She worked hard— she always had. She was great at applying herself to challenges and overcoming them. If that went out of her life—if her job suddenly became easy—wouldn't she become unbearably bored?

She thought about how her ex-boyfriend, Ron, would laugh if he saw her there in such a small town. He'd probably say it was the size of a shoe box—she'd heard him talk about small towns that way before. She could just picture the slightly condescending smirk on his face as he questioned her choices. She squared her shoulders as she drove, determined to not be bothered by what she knew he would be thinking, but the truth was that she was also doubting her choice to come to Blueberry Bay. What if it had been a mistake?

She took a deep breath, telling herself firmly that she came there for a reason. She'd needed a change of pace and she knew that the town could use another doctor. She was determined to run her clinic in Blueberry Bay with the same professionalism that she would have had for any other clinic.

In another minute, she arrived at her destination. She parked outside of Tidal Wave Coffee, taking note of what a cute place it was—she couldn't help feeling a little charmed by it. She got out of her car and went inside, where she was immediately greeted by the rich, earthy aroma of coffee.

She inhaled the smell eagerly and stepped up to the counter to order. There was a man standing behind it who looked as though he'd just come out of the ocean. His wavy, long dark hair looked as though it was still drying after coming into contact with salty waves. He gave her a big smile even though they were total strangers. "Hi. How are you doing?"

"I'm fine," Gwen said curtly. "I'd like a Frappuccino and an americano. Both larges, please."

"You got it." He smiled at her again and began to start on the drinks. Gwen noted that business was apparently slow for everyone that morning—although there were a few people sitting at tables in the open area behind her, there was no one waiting in line after her. The man with the wavy dark hair moved at a reasonable pace, but she wished he would put a little more speed into it. Just because he wasn't in a rush didn't mean that she wasn't, she thought with a squirm of frustration.

The man seemed to notice the way she was pressing her lips together, but instead of speeding up, he started to talk to her again.

"I'm Michael O'Neil, the owner of the coffee shop," he said, his lips curving slightly, almost as if he found her impatience amusing.

"Gwen Dunaway," she said briskly, offering a polite but unenthusiastic smile.

"Are you new in town?" he asked, smiling as he worked on the Frappuccino. "I don't remember seeing you around before."

"I am new in town." Privately she wondered if there were so few people in the town that he knew everyone. That didn't bode well for her. "I just arrived a few days ago. I'm a doctor, I just opened up a private practice not far from here."

"Oh, that's great! Glad to hear it. We could use another doctor here in Blueberry Bay." He grinned at her. "Welcome to our community. Have you gotten a chance to see much of Blueberry Bay yet? It's a great town."

"I'm sure it is." She smiled, inwardly willing him to move a little faster so she could get back to her clinic sooner.

"You should check out the Beyond the Sea dinner cruise as soon as it opens for the summer season. It's run by my fiancée, Caitlin Lewis. It's really spectacular—a gorgeous ship and incredible food. You'll love it—people say it's one of the wonders of Blueberry Bay." He grinned, clearly proud beyond measure of this Caitlin Lewis who was his fiancée. For a moment Gwen wondered what it would be like to be in a relationship like that—with someone who thought the world of her. Her stomach fluttered a little as she wondered if she would ever have someone like that in her life.

She smiled politely. "It sounds very nice," she said. Privately, however, she was dismissing his invitation. She felt confident she wouldn't be checking out the cruise—she couldn't remember when the last time was that she'd done something simply for pleasure. She usually spent her evenings seeing patients or doing research. And just then she was still getting settled into her new place, which was taking up a great deal of her time outside of work. Her life in New Hampshire had centered around her hardworking, driven attitude, and she didn't see herself starting to take time for leisure just because she'd moved to a new place.

"The weather out here is great," Michael continued cheerfully as he started to make the americano. "I know it's a little chilly now, but as soon as it's fully spring out here, you're going to love it. Next time you come here, you should sit outside and enjoy the patio seating. It's a great place to read a book, or just sit and think for a while."

"Maybe," she said, smiling briskly again. Internally, though, she was brushing his suggestion aside again. She didn't have time to sit and soak up the small-town atmosphere. If she was going to read a book, she would rather read it at her desk or in her apartment where she could concentrate properly and take adequate notes.

"Here you are," he said, flashing a cheerful grin as he handed her the drinks. "Anything else I can get you?"

"No, that's it, thanks," she said. She felt impatient to bolt out the door and go back to her clinic. She hated the idea of someone showing up and being told, "Sorry, the doctor is out getting coffee." It would make a terrible first impression.

"See you again soon!" he called cheerfully as she stepped out the door, and she smiled back politely.

She glanced at her watch as she hurried back to her car, holding the cups of coffee. They smelled incredible, and she was glad she'd gone on the errand even though it had lasted longer than she'd wanted it to.

Once she was back inside her car, she took a sip of her drink and her eyebrows lifted in surprise. It was the best coffee she'd ever had.

Hmm, she thought. *I guess Blueberry Bay has its perks.*

She started to pull out into the road just as a truck was backing out of a parking spot across the street. The truck was filled with lumber, some of which was jutting out beyond the back of the truck bed. The driver of the truck clearly didn't see her and was moving with an unreasonable speed.

She slammed her hand on her car horn and the truck stopped just in time. She realized that her heart was in her throat, and she pulled back over onto the side of the road to catch her breath and wait for her heart rate to go down. Even though there had been no accident, she knew it wasn't safe to drive when her emotions were high.

She put her car into park and took a deep breath.

She glanced over at the truck, expecting it to just hurry on its way—but she was surprised to see that the driver had also pulled over onto the side of the road. She watched as a man wearing a black leather jacket hopped out of the truck and hurried across the road toward her.

She raised her eyebrows in surprise. The man stepped up to her window, smiling and waving. She noticed how kind his eyes looked.

"Hi," he said, as she rolled down the window. "I'm so sorry about that."

She blinked, surprised that he'd gotten out of his car rather than simply waving an apology to her and driving off. Everyone in Blueberry Bay seemed to be unusually friendly, she thought.

"Well, no harm no foul," she said. She wasn't entirely sure what to say—she felt that he should have been more careful, but she didn't feel comfortable reprimanding a stranger. Especially such a kind, friendly stranger.

"I guess I'm a little too excited to get all this lumber over to Little Clams. I forgot to check where I was going."

Gwen wondered what Little Clams was— probably some kind of specialty grocery store—but she didn't want to ask questions. She had coffee to get to Heidi and a clinic to run.

"I accept your apology," she said, realizing that she sounded a little cool, but she didn't know what else to say or how to say it. After an awkward pause in which he was still smiling at her, she nodded stiffly.

He held his hand out to her. "I'm Isaiah Dunlap. I'm here making renovations to Little Clams."

She nodded again, blinking a little bit. She didn't know what to say—she couldn't very well say "Welcome to Blueberry Bay" when she'd just arrived herself.

"You must be new around here too," he said, grinning at her.

Her eyebrows lifted. She was surprised that he'd guessed that.

He must be a perceptive person, she thought—and she noted that behind his almost goofy grin, his eyes gleamed with intelligence.

"Yes, I am. I'm the new doctor in town."

"That explains it," he said, his expression slightly mischievous.

"Explains what?" she asked slowly. She thought in a flash of the coffee and Heidi waiting at the clinic that she wanted to get back to—but she felt herself getting drawn into the conversation. She wanted to know what this man was thinking, and why his eyes were glinting like that.

"The people here in Blueberry Bay have an easygoing attitude that you don't seem to have," he said, still grinning.

She had to stop her jaw from dropping. She couldn't believe he would just come right out and say something so forward. He said it in such a friendly way that she couldn't be particularly offended, but she still felt shocked. It was as if he'd taken regular social conventions and turned them upside down, making her question herself.

"I'm here to do my job, not to have an easy time," she said curtly. "Speaking of which, I need to get back to my clinic. It was nice to meet you."

She nodded at him one more time, and he stepped back, still smiling a little. He waved to her as she pulled her car back onto the road and started to drive back toward the clinic.

She squared her shoulders as she drove, starting to question the way other people perceived her for the first time in many years. What had Isaiah Dunlap seen in her that made him say what he did?

He'd never stopped smiling, so whatever he thought of her, it couldn't be too bad, she reflected.

But had she behaved in a way that she shouldn't have?

She thought back over their interaction, realizing that she could have been a little friendlier—but he'd almost hit her car! She could have been downright rude to him, and she hadn't been.

She realized that people in Blueberry Bay must be especially friendly and laid-back, if he was surprised by her curt response under the circumstances.

She arrived back at the clinic and made her way inside, trying to stop thinking about Isaiah Dunlap. She gave Heidi her coffee and the two of them sat down in the waiting room together. Heidi gushed excitedly over how good the coffee tasted, and how excited she was to experience more of Blueberry Bay. Gwen nodded as she listened, thinking to herself that she needed some work to do—she was still feeling restless and jittery. She felt impatient to do something constructive. And, she had to admit, she was finding it hard to not think about Isaiah and wonder what he thought of her.

CHAPTER FOUR

Paige Garner grinned to herself as she began to tidy up her baking station at Flourish Baking School. Around her, her friends were chatting and laughing about how their class had gone—they'd been making soufflés, and many of the students' bakes had turned out terribly. Thankfully, no one had taken it too hard and everyone had laughed good-naturedly about the disasters. Paige's soufflé had turned out beautifully, and her teacher's praises were still ringing in her ears as she put away her ingredients.

"Are you coming for movie night tonight, Paige?" asked her classmate, Sarah, at the door.

"Yeah, sounds great!" Paige grinned. "What are we watching?"

"I don't know, it's Katie's turn to pick out the movie."

"Uh oh," said their friend Steve. "Katie always picks tear-jerkers."

Paige laughed. "Ask her to pick something funny this time, would you?"

"I'll try." Sarah laughed, and she and Steve left the classroom, waving to Paige as they went.

Left alone in the room, Paige started to hum quietly to herself. She felt proud of the work she'd accomplished that day—and all of the work she'd accomplished that semester so far. She was looking forward to the rest of her classes, and all of the things she was going to learn. Even more than that, she was looking forward to graduating. Even though she loved school and she would be sad to leave it, she was itching to get back to Blueberry Bay so that she could start her own bakery there.

Once her baking station was spotlessly clean, she swung her backpack onto her shoulders and left the classroom. From there, it was a short walk across campus and along a few of Providence's sidewalks to her apartment building.

She climbed the staircase up to her little studio, feeling tired but happy. She unlocked the door and pushed it open, breathing deeply of the smell of her apartment. It always had a lingering aroma of flour and sugar because she baked in it so often. She practiced baking at least once a day at home, in addition to her studies at school.

She set her backpack down on the little couch she had placed against the window and walked over to the kitchenette. Resting on the counter was the notebook where she scribbled down all her recipe ideas. She kept it there because she used it so often— that recipe notebook was something that she baked out of almost every day. She wanted to make sure she had all of her recipes perfected before she graduated, so that she could begin to launch a successful bakery immediately.

Leaning against the counter, she flipped through a few pages of the notebook, wondering what recipe she should try to make that night. There was a peanut butter cookie recipe she'd been wanting to tackle, and she decided on that. Smiling and humming to herself again, she went back over to her backpack to get her phone. As she started to boil some water for macaroni and cheese, she called her big sister Josie.

The phone only rang a couple of times before Josie picked up, sounding eager.

"Hey, Paige!" she sang into the phone.

"Hey! I just wanted to call and say hi." Paige smiled as she started to chop up some tomatoes to put in the mac and cheese. "How are you doing?"

"Wonderful!"

Paige grinned. Ever since her sister had gotten married, she'd always responded to that question with "wonderful." "How's Wesley doing?"

"He's extraordinary. It's amazing getting to see him every day."

"No domestic squabbles yet, huh? Even though you're both living in that apartment together now?"

Josie laughed. "We disagree about stuff sometimes, but it's all raindrops and no thunderstorms, if you know what I mean."

Paige chuckled at her sister's metaphor. "Okay, okay. Glad to hear it." She grinned. "So how long is it going to be until I'm an aunt?"

Even though she couldn't see her sister, Paige could just picture Josie's mouth popping open into an "o."

"Come on, you know I'm going to make the absolute best aunt," Paige said, opening the box of noodles to get ready for when the water was boiling.

Josie laughed. "You're right, you will. And we are trying," she admitted. "We do want kids right away."

Paige was thrilled, and she spun around in her kitchen. "I can't wait!" she sang out. "You're going to have an adorable little baby, and I'm going to spoil him or her like crazy. That kid is never going to want for cookies."

Josie chuckled, sounding just as excited as Paige felt. "Not too many sweets, though," she said, and Paige could hear the grin in her sister's voice.

"Oh right, I forgot about how much you care about eating healthy," Paige teased. "Okay. I'll make bran muffins regularly and cookies every once in a while."

"Hey, those bran muffins you made that one time were amazing."

"Oh, man, I forgot about those! I was practicing because I knew we were going to be making them in class here. They were okay."

She grimaced, not being particularly fond of bran muffins herself. Her health-nut sister was another matter.

"They were amazing," Josie insisted. "At least as far as bran muffins go," she admitted honestly.

Paige chuckled. "It's been fun trying all kinds of new recipes here—I've gotten really good at making gluten-free stuff—but I can't wait to graduate so I can just choose all my own recipes. And I can't wait to come back home."

"I can't wait for you to come back home either!" Josie exclaimed. "I'm literally counting the days. Wesley can confirm that."

"You are, huh? Wow, you must really like me." Despite her teasing tone, Paige's heart glowed with happiness to hear her sister's words.

"You know I do," Josie said cheerfully. "We're going to have so many adventures this summer. Boating and hiking and going to celebrations. I'm so excited."

"I'm counting the days myself," Paige confessed, laughing. "It's just a little over a month, and then I'll be going home."

"It feels good to hear you call Blueberry Bay 'home.' I remember when you first came here, you couldn't wait to leave."

"Yeah, that didn't last long." Paige thought with a fond smile of how Blueberry Bay had captured her heart. It had started with her friend Tommy Ryan, and then the women of Blueberry Bay had showed her what a supportive community looked like. She'd worked at Tidal Wave Coffee and sold some of her bakery there. All around her had been people who cared about her and wanted her to succeed—even though she had great friends at school and was having a wonderful time there, it wasn't as great as Blueberry Bay was. She'd had a sense of home when she was there that she'd never experienced anywhere else, and she couldn't wait to go back. Best of all, her sister was there—her repaired relationship with her sister Josie was absolutely one of the best things in her life. "I love our town. And I love you."

"Oh!" Josie cooed. "I love you too."

Paige grinned. "And I can't wait to be back home so I can start really putting roots down. I want to become an aunt, and I want to meet a guy of my own someday—"

"Oh really, now?"

"Shush, of course I do!" Paige waved a hand, her cheeks turning pink. "And most of all, I can't wait to start my bakery. Well, my own business. The actual bakery part will come later."

"You still want to bake for local businesses first before opening up your own shop?"

"I do. That seems like the smartest choice as far as finances go. I should be able to save up a lot of money that way."

"Sounds brilliant to me. And I know you've got it all planned out, in every detail."

"I do!" Paige smiled as she poured the box of noodles into the pot of boiling water. "I really do. I've got so many lists and charts and everything—and I'm practicing and perfecting all my own recipes so I'm ready to hit the ground running."

"I'm so proud of you, Paige. I can't wait to see your plans succeed."

Paige's heart glowed over her sister's words. "Thank you, Josie. I can't wait to see you and Wesley have all kinds of cute babies and move into your dream home together."

Josie laughed. "Me either. Although I have to admit, I'm pretty content with how things are right now. Life feels extra sweet now that he's my husband."

"Aww, cheesy."

"Mm, I'm not sorry. Hey, speaking of sweet things, did you talk to Michael about selling your bakery at Tidal Wave Coffee again once you get back?"

"Not yet! Well, not officially—we talked about it last time I was there and he said he definitely wants me to bake for the coffee shop again. But we haven't discussed the actual business details yet."

"You should—you should talk to him about the drinks he's planning on showcasing over the summer.

Then you can see if you can kind of follow those themes a little with your baked goods."

"Oh, that's a great idea! Thank you."

"Of course! And the other thing is, Caitlin's wedding is coming right up. Do you want me to ask her if she has someone lined up to make the wedding cake yet?"

"Oh, wow." Paige's stomach flopped in nervousness at the thought. A wedding cake was a big deal—she'd made big cakes before, and they'd studied wedding cakes in her classes at Flourish Baking School, but it was the kind of thing that she felt an enormous amount of pressure to get just right. And she was very fond of Caitlin, and of Michael— she would want any cake for their wedding to be nothing short of perfect. "Yeah, you can ask her."

"I can hear how nervous you are. Your voice went up almost a whole octave." Josie chuckled. "Don't sweat it. I know you would knock a cake out of the park, and I know Michael and Caitlin think highly of your baking already. It's up to them. If she says yes, I know you can do it."

"Okay." Paige smiled, still feeling nervous but grateful for her sister's encouragement. "Thanks, Josie."

"Absolutely. Oh, wow, it's later than I thought it

was. I'm still on honeymoon time. I should get going, I've got to start making dinner in earnest."

Paige laughed. "Me too. Talk to you soon?"

"Yes! Good luck with all your classes!"

"Good luck with being married!"

The sisters both laughed again, said an affectionate goodbye, and hung up. Paige set her phone down on the counter and began to grate cheese for her pasta. As she worked, she saw her phone light up with a text from her mother. She grinned and picked it up, reading the text eagerly.

MOM: Hey, sweetheart! How are things going at school?

Paige shut her eyes for a moment, allowing herself to feel a rush of relief and hope. After her mother had been sent to rehab, she had made vast improvements in her life. It was clear that she was taking her sobriety journey seriously, and she was putting in the work to be better.

After Paige had chosen to live in Blueberry Bay instead of return home to continue living with their mom, she'd been worried that her relationship with her mother would fall apart. Instead, the opposite was happening—her mother was becoming more dependable and supportive. Her mother had gone to Josie's wedding, and the three of them had gotten to spend a lot of sweet time together. Things between the daughters and their mother were improving, and it gave Paige a great deal of joy.

She smiled as she texted her mother back, feeling glad that her mother wanted to know about her life. She felt as though she wanted to type out every single detail of what was happening, so that her mother could hear about all of her good news.

PAIGE: Hey, Mom! Things are going great. I just made a successful soufflé earlier, so I'm glad that challenge is in the books! And I just talked to Josie too. Sounds like you might be a grandmother pretty soon!

She knew her mother would respond again in a moment, but for now, she needed to get her food cooked. After dinner, she planned on baking, and then bringing her peanut butter cookies to the movie night with her friends. She set her phone back down on the counter and hummed to herself as she continued her preparations for dinner.

* * *

Isaiah muttered enthusiastically to himself as he laid down materials for the new play structures on the

Little Clams playground. The pieces were painted a bright blue and they reminded him of when he had been a little kid, rushing around being hyper on the playground with his friends.

He stood up straight and stretched, looking up at the clear blue sky. It seemed to be a lighter echo of the blue of the new playground equipment, and he smiled to himself as he thought about how nice the new playground would look on clear summer days.

"Hey, you! Are you hungry?"

He turned and saw his sister, Olivia, walking toward him, carrying a tray of food. He grinned at her and gave her a sideways hug as she reached his side.

"I sure am. How can you read my mind like that?"

"I'm your sister, I grew up alongside your stomach." She laughed. "This is left over from the kids' lunch. I hope you don't mind peanut butter and jelly."

"I love peanut butter and jelly," he said, meaning it sincerely. He picked up the sandwich and took a large chomp out of it. "Oh, thank you. And no crusts. This is sublime."

She laughed as he took the tray from her. In addition to the peanut butter and jelly sandwich, there was a bowl of carrots, a side of ranch dressing, and a chocolate chip cookie.

"You want to sit down on that bench and talk about the renovations while you eat?" she asked, pointing to a wooden bench that was splashed with colors as if several kids had hurled cans of paint at it at the same time.

"Sure. You want some of my carrots?" he offered.

"No, no, you eat those. I already had my lunch."

Isaiah sighed, since he wasn't fond of carrots, but he couldn't help grinning at his sister's playful banter.

They sat down on the bench together, looking out across the playground. It was a sunny day, and the spring was getting warmer, making it pleasant to be outside in the sun. Nearby, birds chirped in tree branches which rustled in a light wind.

"It's a beautiful day, isn't it?" she said, leaning her head back and closing her eyes.

"Just gorgeous," he agreed. "How are classes going?"

"Fun! Except one bad thing happened this morning. I had a kid—well, uh, lose their lunch so to speak, during class this morning, but their parents came to get them and take them home. I've been texting the mom and it sounds like it was just food poisoning or something and the kid will be better soon, so that's good."

"That is good." There was a short pause, and then he said, "If it happened during the morning, wouldn't it be losing their breakfast then?"

She shook her head at him, laughing.

"Well, I hope that kid feels better soon," he said, taking another chomp out of the sandwich. "Now tell me all your hopes and dreams about this playground," he said with his mouth full.

Grinning, she began to tell him where she wanted him to place everything. After he felt clear about all of her instructions for the playground, they talked more about the indoor renovations for the school. Isaiah smiled to hear how enthusiastic his sister was about the school. He was glad that he could be there to help her improve a place that she loved so much.

"Do you think you'll be able to get all that done in time?" she asked nervously.

He laughed. "Of course! Stop worrying about that. Make me a list of what our priorities are, just in case, but that all sounds more than manageable."

She pursed her lips. "Okay. Thanks, Isaiah."

"You still look nervous," he teased.

"Well—" She bit her lip, chuckling. "I know how

optimistic you are. I'm just wondering if maybe you're not really calculating all of the time you're going to need properly. Like, taking trips to bring the lumber here, things like that."

"I already got all the lumber," he said proudly. "I brought it over in my truck the other day."

Her eyebrows lifted in surprise. "I would have liked to see how you managed to get all of that lumber in your truck at once."

"It fit—but I have to admit that while I was transporting it, I nearly had a run-in with the new doctor."

"You got injured?" she asked in concern.

"No." He laughed. "I was backing up too fast and I almost hit her car. Almost!" he added as Olivia's eyes widened.

"Well, I'm glad it was all okay!" Her brows rose, curiosity clear in her expression. "I didn't know we had a new doctor in town. That's great news. What's she like?"

"Very pretty," he blurted, and immediately regretted his honesty when his sister's smile turned into a mischievous grin.

"Oh, she is, huh?"

He felt as though the tips of his ears might be turning a little pink, but he was determined to ignore the feeling. "Just... you know, objectively. She's a woman around our own age, not an old man or anything like that."

"Right. Because the only way to tell me that she's a younger woman instead of an old man is by saying that she's pretty." Her lips twitched as if she was hiding a smile.

He wrinkled his nose at her and kept talking. "She seems like a fish out of water here, I have to admit. She's got 'city' written all over her. You know, she seems on edge and in a constant hurry. That type of person. Everyone in Blueberry Bay is relaxed—people here know how to take things easy. She seems pretty out of place here."

"Well, you're new too. You're also a fish out of water."

"Sure," he said, grinning, "but I'm already blending in with the locals and charming everyone with my pleasant, laid-back attitude."

She laughed. "Yeah, I can't argue with that. I know your charming nature and your jokes have probably won the hearts of the people of Blueberry Bay already."

"See? Even my own sister thinks so. And she's sick of all my jokes by now."

"I'm sure that serious-minded doctor was another

story, though," Olivia pointed out. "I bet she was having none of your jokes."

He chuckled. "Well, I didn't exactly tell her any jokes, but yeah, she didn't seem too pleased. But I can't blame her for being stressed under the circumstances, and she wasn't mean or anything. I don't think she's all bad. She seems interesting—and I expect she'll acclimate to Blueberry Bay before long."

"Well, I hope so. If she's the stressed-out type, she might not give herself the time to really let go and get to know people."

He nodded. "Yeah, but I've decided I want to help her settle in here."

"Oh, really?" Her expression was almost gleeful, and he knew he was going to get teased again in a moment or two.

"What's so surprising about that? We're both new. I figured I could help her feel more comfortable here. And I could maybe help her kind of learn how to take on a more... uplifted attitude."

She arched a brow. "You have a very optimistic way of moving through life. Is it your mission to make sure that everyone else is optimistic too?"

He grinned and dipped a carrot in the ranch dressing before popping it into his mouth. "I don't see what harm it would do. And this doctor seems like the perfect candidate."

"Hmm. I see what you're saying. And the fact that she's pretty has nothing to do with your benevolent intentions, huh?"

He lifted a brow at her. "Who else in this town do you propose that I teach how to be optimistic?"

She nudged him with her shoulder. "That's a good point. And all kidding aside, I think that's a sweet idea—to help welcome her to town. If she's new here, she's probably feeling lonely and out of place. It's always hard to move somewhere new and leave an old life behind."

For a few moments, they sat comfortably side by side, both looking out across the playground. Isaiah ate a couple more carrots, finding that he was enjoying the taste more than he thought he would. He kept thinking about meeting Gwen, and wondering what kind of a person she was underneath her curt exterior.

"I think I'll go over to the doctor's office and welcome her as well," Olivia said after a few moments, smiling. "I'll make something for her. Lemon bars. I make some seriously good lemon bars. That should make her feel welcome."

Isaiah thought privately to himself that it was

ironic that his sister wanted to bake something with a sour flavor for the less-than-sweet newcomer.

And anyway, it's going to take more than sugar to sweeten that woman up, he thought to himself.

Then he smiled. He was up for the challenge.

CHAPTER FIVE

Johanna turned to smile at her boyfriend, Everett Howell, as she cuddled up closer against him. The two of them were outside at night, and she could hardly see him in the darkness, but she could see him enough to know that he was smiling at her with a glow of affection in his eyes. They were out on a hilltop on the edge of Blueberry Bay together, snuggled close together with a blanket around both of their shoulders. It was a beautiful cloudless night, and despite the chilly temperature, she felt warm and cozy next to the man she loved.

They were there to stargaze using Everett's high-power telescope—stargazing was a passion that they shared, and it was something that had brought them together when they were first beginning to date.

Johanna took a deep breath, inhaling the fresh smell of the night air. Overhead, the stars twinkled like jewels, and the wind rustled in the branches of the nearby trees. An owl hooted in the distance, adding a kind of thoughtful music to the beautiful night.

"It's so peaceful being here with you," she said, squeezing his hand. He smelled slightly of fish—something that was rare for him, even though he was a fisherman, but she found she didn't mind in the slightest. She was happy that he'd come straight from working to be there with her. It showed how much he cared about her, and how much he valued their time together.

"It's so peaceful being here with you," he told her, kissing her nose. "A perfect night."

"The weather is perfect too," she said. "Not a single cloud. And maybe it's how happy I feel, but the stars look particularly bright tonight."

He nodded. "Look at Orion. I haven't been able to pick it out so quickly in a long time."

"Maybe it's the sky, or maybe it's that you're an astronomy expert." She nudged him fondly.

"Oh, I don't think I'm an expert," he said, although he sounded pleased.

Privately she thought to herself that he was absolutely an expert. She admired his quick mind so much—and she loved even more that it was paired with a gentle sense of humor. Everett was a kind, considerate man underneath his rough exterior.

As they gazed up at the sky, taking turns using the telescope, they excitedly pointed out various stars to one another.

"Isn't that one beautiful? Just over that belt of pine trees?"

"Yes. Looks bright enough to wish on."

"What would you wish for?" he asked, squeezing her shoulders. "If it really was a wishing star?"

She laughed. "I honestly don't know. I'm so content. I suppose I'd wish for baby Oscar to be healthy and happy, but I'm expecting that to happen without wishing."

"How are Alissa and Dane doing? Are they excited?"

"So excited. Alissa's starting to get tired again, and it's no wonder, considering how soon she's due. I went over to their place with a casserole that Dane loves the other day. They were both very happy about it, and I'm planning on cooking for them again soon."

"That's sweet of you. If they need help with anything—assembling baby furniture, anything like that—let them know that I'm offering to help, would you?"

"I will, thank you." She rested her head on his shoulder briefly. "Dane still has to work so much at the office, and he's worried that Alissa is working too hard as well. He's the one who first told me that she's been a bit tired. I want to help them both out so she feels free to take it easy."

"I'll help you help them. I'm not much for making casseroles, but maybe I can prepare some fish for them. Get some trout or salmon ready to be put into the oven."

"Sounds wonderful!"

"And how are you feeling about the baby's arrival?" He snuggled up closer against her as the wind picked up, blowing cool air across their faces.

"Absolutely giddy," she said, grinning up at the stars. "I can't wait. He's going to be my first grandchild. I'm going to be a grandmother!"

After the words left her mouth, she began to laugh.

"What is it?" he asked curiously. "What's funny?"

"I don't feel like a grandmother," she said, shaking her head. "It's funny that I'm about to become one right when I feel younger than I have in years."

"You do, huh?" he said, his brows rising.

"Mm-hm. You make me feel like a teenager again."

He grinned boyishly. "What makes you feel like a teenager?"

"Oh, those sparkling eyes of yours," she said slowly, resting a hand on his cheek. "And your big strong arms. And the way you make me feel giddy whenever you call me on the phone. I haven't laughed this much in years. You've really done things to my emotions, Mr. Howell."

"I'm honored to make you laugh," he said, placing his own hand over hers. "I love it when you laugh. It's the absolute cutest thing."

She did it again, unable to stop herself. The comic timing of it made him start to chuckle, and soon the two of them were having a laughing attack—his guffaws mixed with her giggles. They held hands and laughed into the night air, startling a rabbit that was nibbling grass nearby.

"Come here, you," he said, grinning at her.

He wrapped his arms around her and leaned his head in for a tender kiss. For a moment, both of them forgot about the stars entirely.

* * *

Gwen jotted notes down in her computer, her fingers typing almost as rapidly as her mind was moving. She paused for a brief moment to make sure she hadn't made any typos, and then kept typing.

She was in her office at the clinic, jotting down notes about the patient she had just seen. She believed firmly in keeping highly detailed doctor's notes, and even though all that had been wrong with the patient was a small cut on her hand, she was still determined to be thorough in her note-taking.

She paused once she'd finished her notes, glancing over them one more time. Nodding in satisfaction, she saved them and then stood up from her computer. She took a sip of coffee as she glanced at the clock, noting that her next patient was due to arrive soon.

She felt as though she was settling into a good groove at her new clinic. There were still not as many patients as she would have liked, but she felt as though her first few days of work in Blueberry Bay had gone well. The people there were kind and welcoming, and everyone she'd met had been friendly and grateful.

She pulled up the file of the patient records for

her next appointment, still standing at her desk instead of sitting. She usually had a great deal of adrenaline while she was working, and she preferred to stand when she could. She frowned in concentration as she read, wanting to be well-prepared for the appointment.

At that moment, there was a knock on the door. Heidi poked her head inside Gwen's office, wearing an expression Gwen couldn't quite read.

"Hey, do you have a second? There's someone here to see you."

Gwen frowned. "My next appointment? I thought it wasn't for another ten minutes."

Heidi shook her head. "This isn't an appointment. It's just a quick social visit. Should I send her in?"

"Sure." Gwen felt a little baffled—who paid a social visit to a doctor in the middle of the workday? More than that, she didn't know anyone in the town who might want to visit her yet.

Into the office stepped a smiling woman with curly brown hair. She was wearing a pair of jean shorts and a sweatshirt, and she was grinning as if she'd known Gwen for years. In her hands was a Tupperware clearly filled with some kind of baked goods.

"Hi," the woman said, her expression warm and friendly. "I'm Olivia Dunlap. I wanted to welcome you to Blueberry Bay."

"Oh." Gwen blinked. She was staring at Olivia, wondering if this Dunlap was related to the handsome male Dunlap who had almost hit her car. "That's very thoughtful of you, thank you," she said stiffly.

"Of course! We're thrilled you're here. I was new in Blueberry Bay once myself—well, more so Whale Harbor. I moved there with my aunt, Marsha Dunlap, and we both love the area—but it's always hard being a new person in a strange place. At least I think so." Olivia flashed a friendly grin at her. "And I know my partner agrees with me—my boyfriend Corey Easton was new here not that long ago. He opened up a souvenir shop in Blueberry Bay. He's got two adorable eight-year-old twins, so it was hard for him to find any extra time to get to know people. Thankfully we found each other, and I helped him get settled here."

Gwen had absolutely no idea what to say. She wasn't used to people who were comfortable sharing their life story at the drop of a hat like this. She wanted to tell Olivia that she didn't need any help settling in—she knew where the grocery store and the bank were located. There wasn't any information about the town that she needed that she didn't already have.

"Here," Olivia said, taking the reins of the conversation again after a few seconds of Gwen's awkward silence. "I baked you some lemon bars." She handed Gwen the Tupperware with a triumphant grin, as if to say, "Just wait until you taste these."

"I—uh, thank you." Gwen mustered a smile. She'd never been handed baked goods by a stranger before. "That's very kind of you."

"These lemon bars are a team effort," Olivia said, laughing. "I misplaced my favorite lemon bar recipe, but my friend Paige Garner came to the rescue and sent me one that she likes. She's an incredible baker —she's studying at Flourish Baking School in Providence right now."

"Oh?" Gwen took a curious sniff, getting a pleasant whiff of the smell of sugar and flour and lemon. "That's very nice. Thank you."

Olivia looked as though she might be trying not to laugh, and in that moment, Gwen felt sure that this woman was related to Isaiah Dunlap—she had the same impish smile that he had. She knew she was acting stiff and a little unfriendly, but Olivia's effortlessly breezy attitude baffled her. After all, they'd never even met before—but here she was dropping off baked goods like they were friends?

"So I texted her and I asked her if she had a lemon bar recipe and she sent me this," Olivia said, still smiling. "You'll love these—they're even better than the ones I usually bake, and that's really saying something. We're all excited for Paige to come back home to Blueberry Bay. She'll be done with school in a little while, and then she's going to start her own bakery here."

"That's nice." Gwen swallowed. Of all the things she'd studied and perfected in her life, being effortlessly friendly wasn't one of them. She was a little unsure of how to deal with such openhearted friendliness—being at ease with strangers wasn't something she considered to be part of her own personality, and she wasn't used to being singled out for the kindness of strangers. She was usually the type to keep to herself, and although she was grateful for Olivia's kindness, she wasn't sure how to reciprocate the same benevolent energy.

"It is. You should be able to buy her stuff at Tidal Wave Coffee soon—she used to sell her stuff there and the rumor is she will again when she gets back home—and then you'll understand why we're all rooting for her. Have you been to Tidal Wave Coffee yet?"

"I have," Gwen said, grimacing as she remembered the almost-collision with Isaiah's truck filled with lumber.

"Did you like it? Oh! That was where Isaiah almost ran into you, wasn't it? He's my brother, and he told me about it. He's so sorry about that."

Gwen offered a feeble smile. "All's well that ends well."

Her heart was starting to thump at the memory of meeting Isaiah—and she told herself it was because it had been a nerve-wracking experience to almost be hit by another car.

"Well, he's really sorry. I hope that other than that stressful experience, you're settling in all right."

Gwen nodded. She wasn't surprised at all that her suspicions were confirmed—Isaiah was Olivia's brother.

Of course he is, she thought. *Everyone must know everyone in this small town, and they're all probably related to each other.*

"It's all right," she said out loud. She wondered if Olivia was bringing the lemon bars as a kind of apology for her brother's driving. "Isaiah already apologized, and it ended up being totally fine. It's all forgotten."

"That's good." Olivia smiled, her eyes warm. "But I know he still definitely wants to make it up to you."

Gwen's eyebrows lifted. She wasn't sure what Olivia meant by that—and she didn't quite know why her stomach fluttered a little at the thought. "That's not necessary."

Olivia chuckled. "That brother of mine is something else. He does everything he does with as much energy as a firecracker. He's a really nice guy, though, and I know he felt bad about not driving as carefully as he should have."

Gwen nodded, glancing at the clock. She still had plenty of time before her next appointment, but she was starting to wonder how she could politely hint to Olivia that it was time for the conversation to end.

"Do you need anything while you're settling in?" Olivia asked. "Everything in your new place works all right?"

"Nothing's broken. Everything seems to be in fine working order."

"Well, if you need help moving furniture—or

finding furniture—let us know. Moving can be a lot sometimes, I know."

Gwen smiled at her, touched by this stranger's consideration. "I have all my own furniture already, and the moving men carried everything upstairs when they arrived with the van. But thank you—that's a kind offer."

"Of course! Got to help a new neighbor settle in. We're all here for each other in Blueberry Bay. Let me write down my phone number for you—you can call me if you need anything."

"Thank you," Gwen murmured, privately thinking that she wouldn't be calling Olivia for any reason, since she was used to solving all her problems on her own. She watched as Olivia reached into her purse, pulled out a small notebook, and scribbled her number down onto it using a pencil that she'd had tucked into her hair.

"There you are," Olivia said, handing Gwen the piece of paper. "That's for emergencies or non-emergencies, like if you want someone to help you navigate the grocery store or help you pick out flower pots. Things like that." She grinned, and Gwen smiled back. "I should probably get going, and I don't want to keep you either."

"Thank you again for the lemon bars. That's very thoughtful of you."

"Of course! I look forward to seeing you around town. Have a good day!"

"You as well. Thank you again."

Olivia waved as she stepped out of Gwen's office. Gwen stood there for a moment, holding the Tupperware of lemon bars and not quite knowing what to do with herself. She opened the Tupperware and looked down at the bars, lost in thought. She smelled the sweet aroma of the baked goods, but she didn't eat one yet.

Everyone is so nice here, she thought, biting her lip. *But I—I can't shake the feeling that I don't belong here.*

She closed the Tupperware lid again and set the bars down on the edge of her desk. She picked up her phone, checking for new notifications, and her stomach flopped in disappointment when she saw that there weren't any.

She wasn't sure why she kept looking at her phone so often. She'd been used to getting texts from Ron regularly, but it wasn't as though she wanted him to be texting her now. She didn't want him to check in with her or try to find out where she'd gone.

She pressed her lips together, feeling the old

familiar knot of frustration rise up in her chest when she thought about Ron. He'd found fault with how dedicated and organized she was—he was always criticizing the orderliness of her life, which was ridiculous. When he'd broken up with her, that was the reason he'd given for why he thought they were go longer going to work out—he'd said that she was too particular, too inflexible.

He benefitted from my hardworking attitude, she thought, looking out the window at the sunny day.

It looked warm outside, but she wondered if the brightness of the sunlight was deceptive, and it was really colder than it had been the day before. Life tended to be like that, she thought. You couldn't trust appearances a lot of the time.

When she'd first met Ron, she'd fallen for him and thought they would do well together. At first, he'd talked a lot about how much he admired her accomplishments. Then it became clear that he wanted to take advantage of her—he barely ever worked, relying on her significantly higher income to keep him afloat financially. Then, in the end, he'd resented her for how hard she worked.

She shook her head, feeling another twist of frustration even though those problems were now in the past. He was the one who had thrown away a good thing—and in the end, she had to be glad that he'd made that choice, as foolish as it was. She knew they weren't right for each other, and that it had needed to end when it did. Perhaps it should have ended much sooner than that—she couldn't remember the last time she'd had any truly loving feelings toward him. She knew that love was more than feelings, it was hard work and effort—but she was glad she'd escaped a relationship in which the other person wasn't willing to put in that work.

She shook her head, feeling herself tense up the more she dwelt on the past. She took a deep breath, checking the time and noting that she only had three more minutes to study her next patient's file before the appointment started.

She went back over to her computer and began to finish reading the file. Her mind moved quickly, and soon she'd managed to shake off the ghosts of the past.

There was no point in looking back, she thought as she stepped out of her office. All she could do was look forward, even though she wasn't sure where her life was going.

CHAPTER SIX

Isaiah ran his fingers through his hair, taking a deep breath. He'd been out on the Little Clams playground ever since dawn, working steadily away at setting up the new playground equipment. Even though the morning was still cool, he was warm and sweaty from working hard for hours.

He walked over to his water bottle, deciding he'd earned a short break. He sat down on the bench on the edge of the playground, letting the cool breeze ruffle his hair. He gulped down half his water bottle in one go, savoring the refreshingly cold liquid. He sighed, rolling his shoulders back a little and taking another deep breath. He drank the rest of the water bottle more slowly, knowing he'd have to go back inside the school soon to refill it.

It was shaping up to be a beautiful day, he thought, looking up at the sky and smiling. It had been a cloudy dawn, but now the clouds were breaking apart and the sun was shining through. His heart felt light, and he felt tired in a good way. He knew he had many more hours of work left in him, and he was excited to get a lot done that day. So far, he was a little ahead of schedule for the renovations, and he wanted to keep it that way—otherwise, Olivia would get nervous, he thought to himself with a chuckle.

Cars were starting to arrive to Little Clams, and kids were hopping out of them and running toward the school, usually with a parent calling after them to walk instead or to be more careful. The kids were shouting to each other and laughing—they looked like a flock of brightly-colored birds hopping along the ground.

I'm so glad I get to spend the spring here, he thought to himself with a smile. *This town is peaceful, but it's never boring.*

He grinned as he watched a group of kids huddled together, staring at the playground and whispering. One of them pointed toward Isaiah, and he waved at them. The kids squeaked and dashed into the school as if Isaiah was a monster who might suddenly bite.

Chuckling, he finished the last gulp of his water. He hadn't had this much fun on a job in—well, maybe not ever. He generally enjoyed the projects he worked on, and he found his work of building things very fulfilling. In spite of that, in the past year or so, he'd started to feel that he needed a change. He'd begun to feel restless—and it wasn't the work itself that he'd become disinterested in. It was as if he'd felt the rest of the world calling to him, calling him away from his hometown in North Carolina. He'd always been fond of the place where he grew up, but he'd been wanting to spread his wings a little, so to speak.

He whistled a little to himself as he stood up and started to walk toward the school, with the intention of refilling his water bottle. His mind continued to wander, jumping back and forth from the past to the future like a kid playing hopscotch. He'd always been optimistic about the future, but now he felt especially excited about it. He was in a place where he was open to wherever life might lead him, and he had a feeling that great things were in store.

As he was opening the back door of the school, he thought suddenly and unexpectedly of Gwen.

Maybe he'd been unconsciously comparing his own optimistic attitude toward the future to her uptight, stressed demeanor.

She'd seemed so serious when he'd met her. Perhaps it wasn't fair of him to assume that she was that way all the time—after all, they'd almost gotten into a car accident—but he'd gotten the impression that she was a no-nonsense, all business type of person.

As he walked along the school hallways, looking for a drinking fountain, he began to wonder how he might be able to lighten her up. He pondered the puzzle energetically—the challenge was something he was looking forward to tackling. He smiled a little to himself as he filled up his water bottle, imagining the serious Gwen starting to laugh and smile. He wondered what he could do to make her feel happy and at ease.

As he was making his way back along the school's hallways toward the playground, he heard someone call his name. He turned, and saw Olivia hurrying toward him, grinning.

"Hey, you," she said, giving him a bear hug. "I was just coming outside to pay you a visit. How's it all going?"

"Great," he said, returning the bear hug. "I was just coming back inside for some water."

"I'll walk you back to the playground," she said. "My teaching assistant is getting the kids settled for a half hour video, so she told me I could sneak out and talk to you for a while."

"I have a feeling you want to talk to me about more than just the renovations," he said, grinning. "You've got that impish look in your eyes again."

She chuckled as they stepped back out into the sunlight. "I might have something to relate that I feel a little extra excited about."

"What is it?" he asked, and then he knew what it was in the next instant. "You went to visit Gw—that doctor?"

"I did." She clasped her hands behind her back and sashayed along beside him. "I brought her lemon bars. I'd misplaced my own recipe, but I asked Paige Garner for one and they turned out even better than my usual ones. Of course they would. Paige is a baking wizard."

"Did she like them?"

She shrugged. "She didn't eat any of them while I was there. I snuck in there in the middle of her workday, so she was probably feeling busy."

"What did you think of her? Does she seem as serious-minded as I thought she was?"

She nodded. "She definitely does. I see what you were talking about. And I like her. She seems like a kind person, but the type that puts kindness into practice in different ways. Like, she spends her days helping people, but seemed uncomfortable with a friendly conversation. She seems like she doesn't really know how to let loose."

"Hmm." He nodded. "Maybe Blueberry Bay will show her how to enjoy the fun side of life."

"Blueberry Bay and you," she teased, amusement dancing in her eyes.

He chuckled, lifting one shoulder in a shrug.

"You know," his sister said slyly, grinning at him, "maybe the two of you will really hit it off. I think she would be the perfect woman for someone like you. You'd provide the fun, and she'd provide the structure. You're so relaxed that you need someone more structured in your life."

His jaw dropped for an instant, and then he collected himself and waved his hand through the air, dismissing her teasing.

"Nonsense," he said. "I'm just hoping to be her friend and tutor her in the ways of optimism. I'm not looking for a relationship or anything like that."

"Just friendship." She gave him a look that suggested she could see right through him.

He wondered if the tips of his ears were turning pink, but he just shook his head at her, laughing.

"I do want to spend more time with her. I want to try to make it up to her for almost hitting her with my truck. I don't want her to think that the people here are inconsiderate, or that I don't take it seriously that I should have been more careful. And I want to get to know her better. She—she seems like an enigma to me. I'd like to try to crack the code of her, so to speak."

She laughed, looking impish. "You do, huh? Well, I warned her that you weren't just going to let the situation go, and you wanted to make it up to her."

"Really? What did she say?"

"Well, I guess your description of a fish out of water really was pretty accurate. She blinked at me a lot. She didn't seem totally opposed to the idea, though."

He grinned. "Did you paint me as some kind of devastated, guilty man who needed to atone for his errors?"

She laughed. "No. I said you were very nice. I think she gets the idea. You're the type to want to make up for things when you make a mistake, and your outgoing nature makes you the kind of person who's always willing to approach a stranger and pull them out of their shell. She'll have all kinds of fun with you. She just doesn't know it yet."

He shrugged, grinning. "Hey, at least she's been warned. Otherwise, me showing up out of the blue with the intent to be friendly might have been too much for her."

She laughed. "You're like an extraterrestrial to her. She needed advance warning of the alien landing."

"Hey, technically we're both aliens. Neither of us is from here."

"Hmm, true." She glanced at her watch, still chuckling. "I should get back in there. Got a lot of kiddos to teach. You text me if you need something, okay?"

"Will do! Have fun with the kiddos."

"Have fun with the power tools."

He grinned. "I always do."

Olivia went back inside, and he smiled to himself as he went back to work. He was looking forward to reaching out to Gwen and getting to know her better.

* * *

"That was probably the best chicken alfredo I've ever had. Thank you, sweetheart." Josie patted her stomach contentedly, glancing at her husband Wesley as they stood in their little kitchen together. "That sauce was incredible."

"The sauce was store bought," he said, grinning. "But thank you for the compliment."

She laughed. "Yes, but you added butter and garlic to it. I saw you. And everything else was cooked just right too."

For a moment, they stood there nuzzling noses, and she felt a rush of contentment.

"I'd better start on these dishes before they get too crusty," she finally said, drawing back and gesturing to the sink.

They'd decided to take turns with cooking and washing up afterward. Since Wesley had cooked their meal for that night, it was her turn to clean up the dishes.

"Let me help you," he said, opening the cupboard to grab some Tupperware for the leftovers.

"No," she protested, tugging on his shirt sleeve. "You made the dinner."

"I know, but now I want to stay here with my wife and help clean up the kitchen." He wrapped his arms around her and rocked her back and forth a little, dancing with her in the middle of the kitchen.

"Okay." She laughed, leaning into the dancing. Privately she vowed to herself that she was going to help him with the dishes the next time it was his turn. "You're trying to win the Best Husband of the Year Award, aren't you?"

"How could you tell?" he teased, and she could feel him chuckling.

"I have my ways," she said. "And I'll give you a tip—right now, the judges are leaning heavily in your favor."

"Wow," he said, dipping her backward. "I hope I win."

Both of them were laughing as he lifted her back onto her feet and they finished doing the dishes together. It didn't take a great deal of time, especially with both of them working together, and soon they were setting the last pot down into the dish drainer.

"I've got to make a phone call, sweetheart," she said, kissing him. "It shouldn't take long."

"To your mom?" he asked, clearly excited for her and the way her relationship with her mother was improving.

She shook her head, smiling. "No, but I did get to talk to Mom yesterday and she's doing great. Tonight

I'm calling Caitlin—I asked Paige if she'd be interested in baking the cake for Caitlin and Michael's wedding. I don't know if Caitlin already has someone lined up or not, but I wanted to ask her."

"That's a great idea," he told her. "Paige would knock a wedding cake out of the park."

"I know! And I'm sure Caitlin feels the same way—but I have to ask her and see if she's already got someone to bake the cake or not. I hope she doesn't— this could be such a great opportunity for Paige. Most of Blueberry Bay will be at the wedding, so it would be a wonderful way of showing everyone what she can do."

"Well, I'm excited to hear what Caitlin says. I have a feeling Paige is going to be making Michael and Caitlin's wedding cake."

She grinned at him and stepped into their bedroom to make the phone call. She dialed Caitlin's number and then sat down on the edge of the bed, smiling a little as she listened to it ring.

"Hey, Josie!" Caitlin's voice said cheerfully from the other end of the line. "How are you doing?"

"Hey!" Josie grinned as she heard her friend's voice. "I'm doing great, how about yourself?"

"Oh, busy." Caitlin laughed. "It's been a lot

trying to plan this wedding—but I'm sure you know all about that! How's married life?"

"Absolutely amazing," Josie said, flopping back on the bed and staring up at the ceiling. "I feel like I'm dreaming."

"Good." Josie could tell from Caitlin's tone that she was smiling. "I'm so happy for you. Wesley is a great guy."

"He really is. And speaking of great guys, how's Michael doing?"

"Wonderful as usual. He's been helping me with all the wedding planning—he's been insisting on that, since he was the one who suggested having a big celebration instead of a simple courthouse wedding. He's been so enthusiastic about the whole thing—and so has Pearl. They're helping me choose joy over stress, if you know what I mean." She laughed again.

"I absolutely know what you mean—and I think I might be able to help you with some of that workload. Or at least, I hope I can. Do you have someone lined up to bake the wedding cake yet?"

"No, I don't—oh! Will Paige have graduated by then?"

"Yes, she will. How would you feel about her making the wedding cake for you guys? She's made wedding cakes before, but only in practice."

"I'm definitely intrigued by the idea. I adore her baking—we all do. Do you think she's up for such a big task, though? There's a lot of people invited to the wedding, so it would have to be a pretty big cake, maybe bigger than what she's made before."

"I know she can handle it." Josie smiled, feeling a glowing sense of pride in her sister. "After all, this is Paige we're talking about. I'm sure she'd practice the cake three or four times before the wedding."

"That's a good point! I know how hard working she is—and no one can argue the fact that she's talented. And besides, I'll never forget the support that I got from our community when I was first starting the Beyond the Sea Dinner Cruise, and I'd absolutely love to help out another aspiring businesswoman. Especially one as dedicated as Paige."

"Thank you! I mentioned it to her already and told her I'd ask you what you thought. She said she's up for it if you still need someone."

"Sounds great. I'll give her a call and we can discuss everything. Michael and I have yet to decide on a flavor, and I bet she can help us with that."

"Definitely. Thanks, Caitlin! I'm really excited about this."

"I am too. I—oh wait, hold on a second." For a

moment, Caitlin stopped speaking, and Josie could hear Pearl saying something in the background. "Oh, I'm sorry, honey," Caitlin said, her voice a little muffled. "Hey, Josie? Pearl isn't feeling well. I should go. I'll call Paige as soon as I get a chance."

"Thank you! I'm sorry to hear that. Tell Pearl I hope she feels better soon."

"I will. Have a good night!"

"You too!"

The friends hung up, and Josie sat on her bed, staring into space. She hoped that Pearl felt better very soon, and that Caitlin decided to hire Paige to bake the wedding cake. Smiling to herself, she stood up and went out into the main part of the apartment to find her husband.

CHAPTER SEVEN

Gwen stood in her office, checking the information for her next patient. It was a little girl, and the form stated that she'd been feeling nauseous and had been running a fever the night before. She pressed her lips together in concern—it was unlikely to be anything serious, but she always felt especially bad for the kids that came in and were sick with something. She noted that the age of this little girl was eight.

She glanced at the clock and decided to head to the examination room right away—it was still five minutes before the appointment, but perhaps this little girl and whoever had brought her would be there early.

She stepped out of her office into the lobby and saw Heidi talking to a smartly-dressed woman with brown hair. Standing beside the woman was a little girl with curly hair who was scrunching her face up as if she didn't feel well.

"Here's Dr. Gwen now," Heidi said, smiling and gesturing to Gwen. Heidi looked down at the little girl with kind eyes and spoke in a reassuring tone. "She's going to make sure you feel better soon, Pearl."

The little girl gazed up at Heidi with wide eyes and a trembling bottom lip. "What if I don't get better in time?" she whispered.

Heidi cocked her head to one side in confusion, but at that moment Gwen stepped in, wanting to make sure the little girl got to sit down somewhere as soon as possible. She looked as though she was sick enough to be uncomfortable standing there like that.

"Hi, I'm Dr. Gwen," she said, shaking the hand of the smartly-dressed woman.

"Nice to meet you. I'm Caitlin Lewis," the woman said, smiling. "I've heard great things about you."

Gwen's face broke open into a smile, and her heart leapt up at the words. Relief swept over her—the clinic getting a good reputation so quickly meant a great deal to her. "Thank you. Why don't you and your daughter come on back to the examination room? You'll feel better in no time at all, Pearl," she said to the little girl, smiling at her.

Pearl offered a wobbly smile in return, and they went into the examination room together. Gwen and Heidi usually did the initial patient check-in together when things at the clinic were slow, so Heidi came into the examination room with them. Pearl sat down on the padded table, looking nervous and holding her mother's hand.

"Now, Pearl," Gwen said, smiling at her, "tell me what you're feeling."

Pearl bit her lip and shrugged, staring at the floor. "My tummy feels sloshy," she said. "I feel like I might throw up. And Mom says I have a fever."

"I took her temperature last night," Caitlin said, "as soon as she told me she didn't feel well. It was 99.8, which is a higher fever than she's had in a long time. I'm mostly worried because she's not talking as much as she usually does." Pearl's mother laughed breathlessly, but she looked nervous. "It really isn't like her, and I'm concerned. She wanted to come see you today and I was more than happy to bring her here."

Gwen nodded, and Heidi typed down notes rapidly on the computer.

"Well, I'm glad you're here, Pearl," she said,

smiling reassuringly at the little girl. "Let's go ahead and take your temperature again."

Pearl's temperature had gone down a little since Caitlin had taken it the night before. Gwen continued to examine the little girl, speaking to her gently and letting her know why she was checking everything that she was. When asked questions, Pearl replied in a muffled voice, staring at the carpet.

"You just have a case of the flu, nothing too bad," Gwen reassured her, once she was certain—although she'd been fairly confident of that diagnosis ever since the little girl had walked into her clinic. "You should be better pretty soon."

"How soon is that?" Pearl asked, biting her lip. Her voice was almost a whisper.

"I can't say for sure, but it won't be too long—" Gwen stopped speaking as she saw the little girl's bottom lip began to quiver. Children were more likely to be emotional when they were worn out from being sick, but it was clear that something was seriously upsetting Pearl.

"What if I miss it?" Pearl said, beginning to cry.

"Miss what?" Gwen asked, glancing at Caitlin in confusion. The little girl's mother was frowning, and then all at once Caitlin's eyebrows lifted in realization.

"Pearl, honey, are you worried you're going to miss the wedding?" Caitlin asked, taking a step toward her daughter.

"Yes," Pearl sobbed, and Caitlin folded her into her arms.

"That's so sweet. But you don't need to worry one bit. You'll be better by then," Caitlin assured her daughter, stroking her hair.

"When is the wedding?" Gwen mouthed at Pearl's mother.

"The wedding is weeks away," Caitlin said to both Gwen and Pearl. "You're definitely going to be all better by then, honey."

"Oh, definitely," Gwen added, smiling. "Don't worry about that."

Pearl took a deep breath, sniffling back her tears. "Okay," she said, offering everyone a watery smile. "Then I won't worry."

"Good," Caitlin said, stroking her head. "You just relax so you can feel better soon."

"You'll definitely be all better by the time the wedding arrives," Gwen said, feeling touched by the sight of Pearl cuddling up to her mother in relief. "Who's getting married?"

Pearl snuffled and pointed a finger at Caitlin.

"Oh! Congratulations," Gwen said, smiling.

"Thank you." Caitlin nodded. "Pearl is from my first marriage, which didn't work out. I'm about to marry Michael O'Neil, the man who owns Tidal Wave Coffee. It's the most popular coffee shop in town. Have you been there?"

Gwen's eyebrows lifted as she made the connection. "I have been there," she said. "I met him. He was telling me about your cruise ship—a dining experience of some kind?"

"Yes!" Caitlin laughed. "He told me once he was going to tell everyone new in town about my dinner cruise and I guess he meant it. That's Blueberry Bay, though, not just Michael—everyone here looks out for each other and helps each other out. That's part of why I love this town so much—the support network is really something. Even our wedding has become a community effort. We've got people offering to help us with things all the time. It's really touching."

Gwen felt her heart soften a little as she heard Caitlin's words. She thought the concept of a community banding together like that was sweet—it wasn't something she was used to. The idea of the people in a town caring for one another like that was a bit of a strange concept to her, since she was used to living in communities where everyone took care of themselves rather than look out for others. She had to admit that the idea of being looked out for by others was nice—it was heartwarming.

"Here's the handout we give to parents when kids have the flu," she said, going over to one of the cupboards in the examination room and taking out a printed information sheet. "She should get plenty of rest and drink plenty of fluids. There's other information here too, about medication and diet."

Gwen handed the sheet to Caitlin, who took it and glanced over it with interest.

"What kinds of foods do you recommend I give her?" Caitlin asked.

"Whatever she can stomach at first, and then try to make what you give her as nutritional as you can. I'd recommend letting her sleep and watch some of her favorite movies today."

"Yay!" Pearl said, suddenly looking excited.

Caitlin and Gwen laughed.

"Thank you, you've been very helpful," Caitlin said, smiling in a friendly way and reaching out to shake Gwen's hand.

"I'm just doing my job," Gwen insisted, returning Caitlin's smile in a more reserved manner. "I hope Pearl feels much better very soon."

"I think she will. She hardly ever gets sick, and

when she does, she usually recovers quickly. I make sure to feed her healthy foods."

"That's very important." Gwen smiled again, and then realized to her surprise that she felt disappointed that Caitlin and Pearl were leaving. She liked the little girl very much, and she had been enjoying talking to Caitlin. "I'll see you both around town, I'm sure."

"See you around town," Caitlin said warmly, and she and Pearl left the examination room. Heidi followed them out so that she could check them out at the front desk.

Gwen lingered alone in the room for a moment, thinking to herself that perhaps it would be nice to get to know the town better. Everyone in Blueberry Bay seemed so kind and pleasant to be around. But she couldn't shake the feeling that she was an outsider—and she didn't know how to become part of a community that she wasn't sure she would fit into. Could she become one of the kind, pleasant people of Blueberry Bay, or would she always feel like someone who didn't quite belong?

I just wish I wasn't the only stranger here, she thought. *I feel like the odd man out, being surrounded by all these folks who know each other so well.*

In a flash, she remembered Isaiah Dunlap—he

was an outsider too, someone who was new to the town and who most people didn't know. She found herself wanting to reach out to him to get to know him better—he at least had something in common with her, since they were both newcomers. And he seemed like a genuinely friendly, fun person.

Unexpectedly, she felt herself flush a little. Then she shook her head, starting to tidy up the examination room. If her goal was to become part of the Blueberry Bay community, there wasn't much point in spending time with him, since he was a stranger in the town as well. A voice in the back of her mind told her that he was sure to get acclimated to the community much faster than she was, but she brushed those thoughts aside.

He's a stranger here too, she thought. *He's not the right person to go to for help with getting settled into the town. Although I have to admit, he doesn't seem like a stranger here.*

She paused in her work, wondering if Isaiah was the kind of person who was at home no matter where he was.

She shook her head, telling herself firmly that it was time to get back to work. She'd spent enough time thinking about things that there was no point in thinking about.

* * *

Alissa snuggled up against the pillows of the bed she shared with Dane, taking a sip of the soothing tea she'd made for herself. She was propped up on the mattress, her glasses resting on the nightstand nearby, surrounded by baby books. She'd been there for an hour already, having finally started taking the gently-given advice of her mother-in-law and husband. She'd been "taking it easy" as they had urged her, and she'd spent a comfortable evening watching a movie with Dane before coming upstairs to bed early.

She and Dane had gotten all the baby books from the library a few days earlier. She wanted to read them out loud to the baby, even though he hadn't been born yet. She'd read once that he could hear the sound of her voice reading to him from inside the womb, and she thought it was a sweet idea. She wondered if he would find the same baby books a little familiar when she read them out loud to him after he'd been born.

She smiled to herself and patted her stomach. "What did you think of that last one, Oscar? It was nice, wasn't it? Just wait till you can see the illustrations."

She chuckled and took another sip of tea. She'd really been enjoying getting some extra rest—she was feeling more relaxed and calm about everything.

Outside, the wind blew in gusts against the house, rattling the windowpanes and hinting at rain. Alissa felt warm and cozy, and now that she'd finished reading all of the books, she was beginning to feel sleepy.

"How's the mother of my child?" Dane said, stepping into the bedroom. He'd been in the bathroom brushing his teeth, and he yawned as he walked over to the bed. He was wearing pajamas that she had bought him for Christmas, and she admired how handsome he looked in them.

"Sleepy," she said, tilting her head up as he leaned down for a kiss.

"Perfect, me too. Except there's so many books in this bed, there isn't any room for me."

She laughed, looking down at all of the baby books that had taken over the bed.

"Poor Dane," she said. "I'll make room for you." She leaned over and gathered up the books into a pile while he climbed into bed beside her.

"Oh good," he said. "That's much better." He snuggled in next to her, wrapping his arms around her. "How are you feeling?"

"Oh, pretty good physically. And excited. So excited. But I feel like I'm getting more jittery about Oscar's arrival all the time. What about you, sweetheart?"

"I'm getting more jittery too," he said, laughing. "It feels like cramming for a test—I want to be totally ready. I want to know everything there is to know."

She laughed. "Yes, that's exactly how I feel! I feel like I've been studying how to be a parent harder than I ever studied anything for school."

Outside, the wind picked up and droplets of rain began to splash against the windowpanes. She sighed in contentment and took another sip of tea, offering the cup to Dane.

"Thanks, sweetheart." He took a sip. "Mm, that's interesting. Tastes like it must be very good for you."

She laughed. "It's supposed to be."

"Do you think we'll be more ready for baby Oscar if we drink more tea?" he teased, taking another sip before handing the cup back to her.

"I expect so," she said, winking.

For a moment, they sat there smiling at each other.

"But no matter how ready we think we are, I'm sure baby Oscar will still manage to surprise us," he said, chuckling.

"That's very true." She snuggled down against the pillows and grinned up at him.

"So the best we can do is be flexible and support each other," he said, taking her hand and stroking her fingers with his thumb. "We'll figure everything out as we go along."

"I promise to do that with you," she said, kissing his hand.

"I promise too," he said, smiling at her. "I don't mean to sound over-confident, but I think we're going to make great parents."

"I think we will too," she said, sighing happily. "We already love him a lot and I know we're going to do our best. That's all anybody can do, really."

"And we'll make sure he drinks tea," Dane said solemnly.

She leaned her head back, a soft laugh falling from her lips. Then she curled up against him as he reached for one of the baby books curiously.

"You want to read to Oscar?" she asked.

"I'd love to," he said. "Are you ready to hear about the very sleepy sloth, Oscar?" He leaned over, pressing his ear to Alissa's stomach. "He says yes."

She chuckled again as Dane began to read the book out loud. She felt a wave of peace and sleepiness wash over her as she lay there cuddled up next to her husband, listening to him read a story out loud to their baby. She still felt jittery about becoming a mother, but she felt much better about it knowing that she would have this wonderful man by her side.

CHAPTER EIGHT

Isaiah grunted a little as he lifted playground equipment pieces and started to carry them over to where he was going to set them up. It was the middle of the afternoon, almost the end of his workday, and he was beginning to feel tired.

He felt proud of the work he'd accomplished that day. He looked across the half-built playground, smiling in satisfaction. It really did look nice—he knew the kids were excited about getting to play on it. He'd heard some of them saying so, and Olivia had told him that they talked about it a lot inside the school.

He glanced at the red brick building and grinned. "It'll be done soon, kiddos," he said, even though none of them could hear him. Every once in a while, he caught sight of one of the kids watching him from one of the upstairs windows—they usually ducked out of sight immediately when he spotted them as if he was some kind of wild man.

He was looking forward to the end of the school day, when all of the kids got picked up by their parents. He enjoyed watching them scamper and run along the sidewalks, excited to go home. He found the sight of them endearing and uplifting. A few of the more outgoing kids had become his pals, and they would stop and say hi on their way to the cars.

And after that, he thought with relish, *I'm done for the day.*

He couldn't stop thinking about what he wanted to do after work—he'd rented a jet boat for the remainder of his time in Blueberry Bay, and he was itching to get out onto the water. He loved boating and being on the ocean, and today was a perfect day to go out. It was warmer outside that day than it had been earlier in the spring, and he had beads of perspiration along his hairline and dripping down the back of his neck. He kept thinking about getting out onto the water and feeling the cool breeze rush against his face. He wanted to drink a cold beer and catch the sunset—he knew getting out on that boat was going to feel so good after working hard all day.

Soon the bell rang, and kids started to pour out of the school like a colorful river. His pals raced up to the playground.

"Hey, Isaiah!" called out the first one, a red-headed kid named Mikey. "How's it going?"

"Pretty good. What do you think of the new swing set?"

"It looks awesome," said a girl in pigtails named Annie. "When are you going to be done?"

"Soon," he promised, and then car horns honked and the kids waved at him and took off. He smiled as he watched them go. He glanced at his workload—he'd been planning on stopping after the last bell, but he told himself he'd get one more thing done that day. The kids were so excited about the playground —maybe he could finish it for them a little faster than he'd planned.

He went over to a pile of metal parts that he hadn't had a chance to sand yet.

It'll be easier to sand these once they're up, he thought. *If I'm careful, I'll be okay. I'll get a couple more pieces set up before going home today.*

He reached down and picked up a long metal piece that was fairly heavy. He was careful to touch the smooth parts of it, since there were jagged metal shards poking out of it here and there. As he was carrying it over to where he wanted to set it up, he stumbled on a tool that he'd foolishly left lying on the ground, and the metal piece slid down in his hands.

"Ah!" he exclaimed, feeling a sharp protrusion of metal slice through the palm of his hand. He dropped the metal piece and looked down at his hand. Bright red blood appeared swiftly in a line along his palm.

"Well, that's not good," he murmured, looking down at it calmly.

It stung badly—but what he was most worried about was how much he was bleeding. He wouldn't be able to continue working until he got his hand cleaned up and bandaged.

I'm sure it's nothing, he thought. *Doesn't seem like that deep of a cut. But I'd better get this cleaned up before I keep working.*

He started to walk toward the school, keeping his injured hand closed in a fist to try to prevent more bleeding. It hurt, but the pain wasn't terrible. He knew there was a first aid kit in one of the staff bathrooms, so he decided to stop there and tend to his cut.

As he was walking along the hallways of the school, Olivia turned the corner and grinned when she saw him.

"Hey, you," she said. "How was your—oh no!"

He chuckled. By that point, he was holding his uninjured hand over the other to keep it from bleeding too much, but his fingers were bloody enough that Olivia was able to see clearly that he'd been injured. "I'm okay," he said. "Just on the hunt for a first aid kit."

"What happened?" she asked in concern, falling into step beside him and trotting along at his side. "A tool cut you?"

"No," he said, shaking his head. "I was foolish enough to try building with pieces I haven't sanded yet. I got sliced by a metal shard."

"Oh, Isaiah," she clucked sympathetically, looking down at his hand with a frown. "I hope it isn't too bad. I'll help you clean it up and bandage it."

"Thanks. I'm sure it's not too bad," he said, smiling at her.

A few moments later, they reached the staff bathroom that had a first aid kit. Isaiah washed his hands in the sink while Olivia opened the kit and got out alcohol wipes and a gauze bandage.

"Okay, let me see it," she said, tearing open the alcohol wipe's packaging.

He laughed and held out his hand. "You sounded just like Mom when you said that."

She grinned, and carefully began to sanitize his cut. He winced, sucking in his breath. It hurt more than he thought it would, and she noticed his reaction.

"This looks deep, Isaiah," she said, pressing her lips together. "And look at how much it's bleeding again already. I think you might need stitches, and—"

He let out a grunt as a sudden shock of pain went through him. Part of the cut hurt a great deal more than the rest of it.

"And I think you might have a metal sliver in here," she said, peering down at his cut in concern. "You need to go to the doctor right away."

"The doctor?" he protested. "Olivia, it's just a cut. I'm sure it'll be fine."

She shook her head firmly. "Absolutely not. I'm not having you get some kind of infection while you're working on something I asked you to do. This needs proper care and attention so it doesn't get worse. You are going to the doctor and that's final."

"Now you really sound like Mom," he said, grinning.

She laughed. "Good. Hopefully that's enough to convince you to go get this cut checked out."

"What if I just keep an eye on it for a while, and—"

"Isaiah!"

"Okay, fine."

She breathed a sigh of relief. "You want me to drive you there?"

"Yeah, if you want. Although I could probably walk there from here, it's not that far."

"I'll drive you," she said. "Let's leave right away, as soon as I finish taking care of this cut."

A few minutes later, he was sitting in the passenger seat of Olivia's car, and she was pulling up to a little red brick building in the middle of one of the gift store areas of town.

"What are we—oh, you're taking me to *that* doctor, huh?" All of a sudden, his stomach did a somersault.

Olivia cocked an eyebrow, glancing over at him. "She's very nice and she knows what she's doing. And besides, she's closer than the hospital."

He gave her a look, and then stuck his tongue out at her for good measure. She grinned at him.

"I'll park the car and then wander around and shop while I wait for you," she said. "Text me when you're done?"

"I will. Thanks, Olivia."

"Of course!"

He got out of the car and started to walk toward the clinic. Olivia had bandaged his cut, but it was still bleeding so much that the bandage was red, and it hurt whenever pressure was applied to it. He was glad he hadn't had to drive himself—that would have been tricky.

He felt a flutter of nervousness as he stepped through the door of the clinic, but he told himself that he was being silly. A smiling young woman sitting behind the reception desk greeted him.

"Hi. Do you have an appointment?"

He held up his bandaged hand. "Nope. This was unplanned."

"Oh my goodness," she said, standing up. "Dr. Gwen is just doing some paperwork in her office. I'll take you into the examination room and then send her right in."

"Thanks," he said.

The nurse led him into a small, clean examination room with mint green walls and a little window looking out over a back garden. It was decidedly the most pleasant doctor's office he'd ever been in, he thought.

"It won't be long at all," the nurse assured him, and stepped out of the room.

A minute later, the door opened and Dr. Gwen stepped inside. He was immediately struck by how pretty she looked—and then he noticed how blank her expression was.

"Hi," he said, grinning at her. "Remember me?"

She nodded, stiffly. He couldn't blame her for being less than enthusiastic to see him, considering what their last interaction had been. She looked immediately at his hand, frowning at it in a clinical way.

"What happened?" she asked.

"Well," he said, lifting one shoulder wryly, "I'm building a playground for Little Clams, and I decided that it wouldn't be any fun if I didn't try to impale my hand while I was at it."

She looked at him with a deadpan expression and blinked a couple of times.

"Do you ever laugh?" he asked, grinning. Then his voice got a little quieter. "Or are you still annoyed with me for almost backing into you?"

"Let's get your hand cleaned up," she said, ignoring his question as if he hadn't asked it. She took his hand and began to unwrap the bandage carefully. "How long has this been on?"

"Less than half an hour. It's a fresh cut."

"Mm, you're bleeding a lot."

"Do you think I'm going to make it?" he asked, teasing, as she picked up a metal tool that looked like some kind of medical grade tweezers.

"I think you have a small chance of survival," she said, her lips twitching a little as she brought the tweezers close to his cut.

He laughed, cheered by the fact that she was bantering with him and even looked like she was holding back a smile. In the next moment, she pulled a small metal sliver out of the palm of his hand.

"There," she said briskly. She examined his hand closely for a few moments. "That's the only splinter, so that's good news. Unfortunately, you will need stitches."

She began to safely dispose of the splinter, and he watched her in admiration. She was clearly very good at her job—quick and efficient. He wondered if maybe she'd only been bantering with him to distract him from the pain of having the splinter removed.

"Don't worry, Doc," he teased, "I'm pretty tough. I can handle some stitches."

"I'm sure you can," she said. "And thankfully, the cut isn't very long."

She sanitized his cut again and began to apply the stitches. It was painful, but he braced himself and tried to focus on other things.

"So, Dr. Gwen," he said, trying to distract himself by talking to her. "Tell me about yourself. What brought you to Blueberry Bay?"

"Well," she said, and he didn't know if she was frowning in concentration or because she didn't really want to answer the question. "I'm from New Hampshire. I had a practice there, which was very successful."

"Huh." He smiled at her as she talked, despite the fact that he was in pain. "Why did you leave it?"

She hesitated, and then said, "I felt it was time for a change."

He cocked his head to one side curiously. She didn't sound particularly enthusiastic about that change—when he looked toward the future, all he felt was eagerness. Her attitude was clearly one of reluctance. "You seem like you're not very excited about the change, though."

For a moment, she paused and gave him a look. It was slightly reprimanding, but mostly surprised—she seemed taken aback that he would be so forward with her, since the two of them were still technically strangers.

"I had a life plan, and then it was altered," she said. "I think that's always a little frustrating."

"I bet it had to do with a guy," he guessed without thinking.

Her expression froze over for a moment, making it clear that his guess was correct. Inwardly he kicked himself for being insensitive, and for a moment, neither of them said anything. He couldn't help wincing a little as she continued to stitch up his cut.

"I guess you're probably thinking that you can tell why he left me," she said dryly, finishing up the stitches briskly.

His jaw dropped. "What?" he protested.

She glanced at him, and he couldn't read her expression—but she almost looked curious. "Well, what are you thinking?"

"Not that," he said without hesitation. "I would never be a jerk like that. Besides," he added hurriedly, not wanting her to misinterpret his words, "I think you're very nice."

"But I'm sure you have theories about why he left me," she said, sanitizing his stitched-up cut. Her tone was playful, but he knew from the look in her eyes that she was hurt about what had happened to her, and she truly wanted to know what he was thinking.

"I do have a theory about that," he said, looking her right in the eyes. "My theory is that he's an absolute fool."

Her lips parted and she blinked a couple of times. He saw her cheeks flush slightly, and she turned away, seeming to not know what to say. She moved a bit awkwardly as she bandaged his hand again and then washed her hands at the sink.

"Well, thank you," she said finally.

"Of course," he said, grinning at her. "If there's one thing you can always trust me to be, it's honest."

"What else can I always trust you to be?" she asked, smiling slightly as she dried her hands. There was a teasing glint to her eyes, and he liked it. He liked it a great deal.

"Oh, well, charming and fun to be around," he said, chuckling. "And generally optimistic."

"Hmm." Her smile became a little wider.

For a moment, the two of them didn't say anything. He sensed that there wasn't anything more she had to do for him—after all, his hand was all stitched up and bandaged—and he was surprised that she hadn't told him yet that it was time to leave. He was getting the impression that she didn't want their conversation to end quite yet. He grinned, liking the idea that maybe she didn't want to stop talking to him. It was a good sign. It meant that she was warming up to him despite the cool attitude she'd had earlier.

For a moment, he considered asking her if he could stay a little while longer and keep talking to her. His lips parted, ready to ask the question, and then he stopped himself. He didn't want to push his luck.

"Well, I guess I'm all set then, aren't I?" he said, standing up and smiling at her.

"Yes, you are." She smiled briskly back. "Have you had a tetanus shot recently?"

"Yeah, not too long ago."

"Good. Then Heidi will give you a print-out on wound care at the front desk. Be sure to keep your cut clean and try to keep too much pressure off it. It should heal fairly quickly, as long as you don't do anything to make it worse."

"Don't be stupid, got it," he said, giving a playful nod.

She laughed a little, and he grinned at her.

"Thanks for stitching me up," he said, reaching out with his unbandaged hand to shake hers. "I appreciate it."

"Of course." Her tone was a little clinical, but her eyes were decidedly warmer than they had been when he'd first arrived. "Call us if something goes wrong."

She stepped out of the examination room and started toward her office. He watched her go, smiling quietly to himself. He hoped that he would get the chance to see her again soon.

CHAPTER NINE

Michael tapped a pencil against his bottom lip, staring down at the small notebook that lay open on the counter in front of him. He was at Tidal Wave Coffee, surrounded by the familiar, rich aroma of coffee and the sound of people laughing and chatting as they drank their beverages. There was a lull in customers, as there usually was in the early afternoon, and he'd decided to use his downtime to work on his wedding vows.

"No, that's not right," he muttered, scratching out the sentences he'd just finished writing. He exhaled in frustration. That had been his seventh attempt at writing out his vows, and he was becoming increasingly frustrated that he couldn't put his feelings into words. He kept making an attempt and then not liking what he had written.

Sighing, he tucked the pencil back behind his ear and started to stare into space. His mind tried to piece together what it was he wanted to say in his wedding vows to Caitlin, but he felt like he was grasping at straws. He knew what his feelings were—but however he tried to phrase those feelings, the words either came out sounding too cheesy or not expressive enough.

At that moment, the front door to Tidal Wave Coffee opened, and Willis Jenkins stepped inside. Michael smiled as soon as he saw the older man—Willis owned The Crab, one of Blueberry Bay's most popular restaurants, and he was a good friend despite his quiet, somewhat gruff demeanor.

"Welcome in," Michael said to the other man with a smile. "You here for some coffee?"

Willis rubbed his hands together. "What else?"

"I seem to recall you buying some bakery here now and again," Michael teased, turning a thumb toward the glass display case, which featured a pleasant array of baked treats.

"That was when Paige was baking for you," Willis joked back. "Come to think of it, though, a muffin might be nice. One of those blueberry almond ones."

"You got it. And a cup of coffee?"

"Black, please."

"Perfect." Michael smiled and got to work putting together Willis's order. "You on a break at The Crab?"

"I am—got to take a break at some point in the day. I've got one of those kids cooking right now. Makes me nervous, but she is good at it."

Michael chuckled, knowing that "kid" could be anywhere from eighteen to thirty-five. "I'm sure it'll work out great. And hopefully this coffee helps perk you up."

"I'm sure it will." Willis smiled, and then he glanced down at Michael's notebook, which was still lying open on the counter. "What are you up to?"

Michael grimaced good-naturedly. "More like what I'm trying to do. I'm trying to compose my wedding vows for my and Caitlin's wedding."

"You are, huh?" The older man's face lit up in a huge grin. "That's so exciting, Michael."

"I wish I could just enjoy the process. I'm really struggling. I know how I feel about her, and how much I love her, and how much I want to make sure I'm a good husband to her—but I'm having trouble putting all of that into words. I don't know how much to say, or how to say it."

"Wedding vows are tricky—you're not just talking to her. Ultimately, you're also talking to everyone at the wedding. You're making a promise to her and they're your witnesses. So whatever you say to her needs to be personal to the two of you and your relationship, but it also can't be so personal that the people watching misunderstand what you're saying."

"Exactly." Michael grinned at him. "I'm getting stuck between sounding too cheesy and feeling like I'm not doing what I have to say to her justice. You got any advice for me?"

Willis smiled. His eyes took on a faraway, sentimental look, and Michael felt sure he was thinking about his girlfriend, Marsha Dunlap, who he'd rekindled a relationship with recently after spending many years apart from her. "You have to reach out and grab love—you have to be brave enough to reach for it and grab it. Making a marriage vow is like that reaching out and grabbing—you're telling everyone else and each other that you're determined to make your relationship last. I almost lost out on love, and it was difficult to find that courage to reach out and take hold of love. You both have already made it to this important point—you're ready to make vows to each other. That's the most important step. Now the trick is keeping that flame alive—fighting for it, so to speak. Lasting love is both grand and simple." He smiled as he talked, and Michael couldn't help smiling too. It was a long time since he'd heard Willis say this many words at once, so it was clear that what he was saying meant a great deal to him. "Marsha makes me feel like I'm the luckiest man in the whole world, and sometimes the way I love her fills me up so much it's like I'm going to burst. Sometimes it's grand like that. Other times, it's simple. It's just normal days, made of hours strung together, and all those hours are filled with little details. Sometimes love has its big, grand moments like getting married, but a lot of it is just the day-to-day stuff. Little things that don't feel important, but ultimately, they are."

"Choosing someone every day, over and over again," Michael said, smiling and feeling a kind of sweet ache in his chest. He knew the feeling Willis was talking about, of feeling like there was so much love in him he was going to burst.

"Exactly." The older man nodded. "Remembering that even through the bad days, they make your life so much better than it would be without them. We're all human, and sometimes marriage is hard. But what you want to say to Caitlin and all your family and friends through your marriage vows is that you're going to keep choosing her every day, to keep that flame alive—not only because of how much you love her in the grand moments, but because of how much you love her in the little moments too."

As Michael listened to his friend, he felt as if the spark of inspiration had been lit in him. His mind was suddenly filled with thoughts of how much Caitlin had made his life better. He felt that he couldn't wait to start writing down all of the sentences that were suddenly in his mind.

"Wow, thank you, Willis," Michael said, hurrying to fill Willis's coffee cup. He didn't mean to nudge the older man out the door, but he felt eager to get back to writing. "That helps me a lot."

"I saw how fast you made that coffee. Trying to get rid of me now, huh?"

Michael laughed, and Willis laughed with him.

"Stay as long as you like," Michael said, handing the owner of The Crab a muffin wrapped in wax paper and a cup of steaming coffee. "But I'm going to start writing now. You can help me edit as I go, if you want." He grinned.

"I'm sure you've got it covered," Willis said, chuckling. "Besides, I should get back to The Crab. I like to take my breaks there just in case something starts on fire—literally or figuratively speaking."

"I hear that." Michael smiled and waved as Willis started toward the front door.

"Let me know how it goes," Willis urged him. "Call me if you get stuck again."

"I will," Michael said warmly, touched by his friend's thoughtfulness.

Willis nodded a goodbye, since his hands were full, and stepped out of Tidal Wave Coffee. With a grin, Michael took his pencil out from behind his ear and began to scribble down sentences in a hurry. He planned on running what he wrote down by Willis when it was done—but he knew he wasn't going to need any help composing it anymore. The words were spilling out of him now, and he knew exactly what he wanted to say.

* * *

Isaiah grinned to himself as he stepped back and looked over the work that he'd accomplished on the playset at Little Clams. His cut hand still hurt a little, but he was able to use it, although he was favoring his other hand more. He'd been working hard all day, continuing to set up the playground with all of the fun new equipment he was building.

The students had left about half an hour earlier, but he still felt like pressing on. It was a perfect day outside—balmy, sunny, with a fresh wind off the ocean that smelled vaguely of flowers. He'd been enjoying being outside all day, and despite the way his hand ached a little, he was eager to get a little more work done.

"No more shortcuts though," he muttered, chuckling to himself. "From now on, I'm making sure I sand everything before I try to set it up."

He continued to work for a while longer, whistling under his breath and feeling the wind ruffle his hair. He was just standing up after securing a blue-painted pole into the ground, when he heard someone call his name. He turned toward the school and saw Olivia and his aunt Marsha walking toward him.

He hurried over to them, grinning. "Well, this is a nice surprise," he said, folding his aunt into a hug. "Are you here to visit Olivia?"

"I'm here to visit both of you," his aunt replied cheerfully. "Olivia's been so excited about the work you're doing here, and I wanted to come see it for myself."

"And in addition to that, we're here to kidnap you," Olivia said, playfully punching his shoulder. "It's time for you to stop and come get dinner with us at The Crab."

"Sounds good to me," he said, grinning. He'd wanted to keep working a little longer, but he knew that it was always more important to spend time with loved ones if work could get done another time. His stomach grumbled, and they laughed. "My body agrees with me," he said. "It's time for some food."

"First I want to see this playset," Marsha said, looking at the work that Isaiah had done with a spark of pride in her eyes. "Tell me all about what it's going to look like when it's completed."

"But it is completed," he teased, pretending to be hurt. Olivia punched his shoulder again and he laughed. "I'm kidding, I'm kidding. But it is getting there. Let me give you the tour, Aunt Marsha."

He walked with both of them through the center of the play area, explaining what he needed to finish and what structures really were complete. Olivia's eyes were shining as she looked at everything—he knew how excited she was for the kids to have their new playground. He felt just as excited as she did—it really was going to be a nice play area, much better than what the kids had had before.

"Well done, Isaiah," Marsha said warmly. "The kids are going to be thrilled."

"Yeah, I think so," he agreed as they started to walk away from the school. "They talk about it all the time."

The three of them strolled along the sidewalks of Blueberry Bay, catching up on everything. Isaiah wanted to know all about how his aunt was doing, and how her relationship with Willis was going. He thought it was cute how she blushed like a teenager when she talked about Willis.

The Crab wasn't too far of a walk from Little Clams, and they reached it in a few minutes. They were soon seated at a table by the window, and Isaiah took a deep breath of the incredible savory smells that filled the restaurant. Around them were the sounds of people laughing and talking, and the clinking of glasses and silverware.

"Oh, there goes my stomach again," he said, laughing as his stomach growled loudly. "I'm ready for some fish and chips. With clam chowder to start."

"That sounds delicious," Marsha said, smiling. "I think I'm going to go with the crab cakes. Willis makes the best crab cakes I've ever had."

Olivia grinned. "I think I'll just ask for a surprise meal. Everything here is good, and I'm not allergic to anything, thankfully."

"And you're not a picky eater anymore," Isaiah teased. She threw her napkin at him.

Their waitress stopped by to take their order and she grinned when she heard that Olivia wanted a surprise. "Sounds good. We'll get your food back out here in a jiffy."

She started back toward the kitchen, and Isaiah took a long drink of water. It had been a rewarding but tiring day, and he was excited to rest and eat some amazing food.

"How's your hand?" Olivia asked him, looking in concern at his bandage. "Any better than it was this morning?" Before her classes had started, she'd stopped by where he was working to say hi and check on him.

"About the same," he said, shrugging. "But at least it's not worse. The pain isn't too bad, and I'm glad that I can still use it, you know?"

"Just be careful, okay?" Olivia said, looking worried. "I know you like to do the thing where you're so optimistic you stop being careful."

He laughed. "Guilty. But the doctor did tell me I could use it as long as the pain doesn't get worse. All

I have to do is change the bandage regularly, and soon I'll need to go back there to get the stitches out." He pretended to shudder.

"Speaking of the doctor," Olivia said, drawing the words out. "Were you able to warm Gwen up a little?"

"Maybe a little bit," he said. "She made a joke or two. She still seems pretty reserved though."

"Was she all business, or did you get a chance to talk to her a little?"

"I did, while she was putting these stitches in." He remembered sitting in Gwen's office, and the careful, dexterous way in which she'd worked on his cut. For a moment, it was as if he could feel her hand on his again. "I found out a bit more about what brought her to Blueberry Bay."

There was a short pause, and then Marsha prompted, "What was it?"

"She's looking for a fresh start after a relationship ended." Isaiah hesitated, wondering how much he should share. "Sounds like the guy was a total fool—he broke up with her."

"Oh?" Olivia asked, raising her eyebrows. "That makes him a total fool, huh?"

Isaiah threw his napkin at her, and she caught it.

"But honestly, I'm sorry to hear that," Olivia said,

handing him back his napkin calmly. "It must have been a rough breakup if she felt the need to move somewhere new."

"That's hard," Marsha said sympathetically. "I hope she finds healing here. Blueberry Bay is a great place to get a fresh start."

"True," Olivia said. Her eyes danced with something mischievous as she pointedly added, "Hopefully she can forget all about her ex here."

"I think her ex must have been an idiot," Isaiah said. "She seems to be kind of insecure about herself because of what he said to her when he was breaking up with her."

He thought about what he'd told her during their conversation at the clinic—that her ex was a fool for breaking up with her. He'd meant it. She might be a bit rigid sometimes—even coming off as prickly now and again—but even though he didn't know her well yet, he could tell that she was also smart and funny, and that she had an innate empathy and kindness. He got the sense that she was a great person, and she tried hard to do things a certain way because she cared about them being done well, not because she was self-centered.

"Knowing that she came here because she's trying to get over heartbreak makes me more determined to help her loosen up and enjoy the town," he said, feeling excited about the prospect.

"I love that idea," Marsha said. "You can help her find healing by showing her all the things Blueberry Bay has to offer. And who knows? Maybe she has a new romance in her future. Maybe you do too."

He felt himself blushing a little, and he shook his head, laughing. "I know what you're getting at. Olivia has already been teasing me about that. I think Gwen is a great person, and I hope she has a great time here, but I'm not looking for a relationship right now."

"Doesn't mean you're not going to find it," Marsha said gently, smiling at him affectionately. "I found love when I was least expecting it. I wasn't looking for it at all. And yet here I am, and I couldn't be happier."

"I wasn't looking for love either," Olivia said. "But then Corey appeared in my life, and I knew there could be something really special between us. I think you might be experiencing that same thing right now."

"Or it could just be that my darling aunt and sister want me to find romantic love, so they're trying to turn a nonromantic situation into a romance," he said, shaking his head at them and smiling.

Their food arrived, and soon their conversation turned toward other topics. Their meals were delicious, and Isaiah savored the rich flavor of his food. He listened to his aunt and sister talk as he ate, thinking to himself that it was the best clam chowder that he'd ever tasted.

As he sat there eating, his mind wandered back to Gwen, and what Olivia and his aunt Marsha had said about finding unexpected love. He kept telling himself that nothing of that sort was going to happen, but he couldn't help wondering what it would be like to find love like that. A surprising kind of love—the kind you weren't looking for. He had a feeling it would be a very exciting experience.

CHAPTER TEN

Caitlin glanced up at her daughter Pearl and pressed her lips together. Caitlin was sitting at the dining room table, catching up on bills, and she had a clear view of her daughter, who was curled up on the couch propped up by pillows, watching one of her favorite movies. Pearl was giggling and happily drinking the smoothie that Caitlin had made for her.

Caitlin smiled to herself and went back to looking at the bills. Her mother radar was going off —it had been a couple of days since Pearl had been to the doctor, and she seemed to be doing much better. Caitlin was beginning to suspect that her daughter was just milking her time on the couch, since being sick meant that she got to have more screen time than usual. Pearl had clearly been enjoying her time resting and being a couch potato, and Caitlin had a feeling that she was going to feel as right as rain as soon as something interesting happened.

As if to confirm Caitlin's suspicions, at that moment, someone knocked on the front door.

"What's that?" Pearl asked, sitting up and looking perky. "Is it a package?"

"We'll have to see," Caitlin said as she stood up and started toward the front door. Through the front windows, she could see a delivery man walking back toward his truck.

She opened the front door and saw a cardboard box resting on the doormat. She saw the name of the online dress company that they'd ordered Pearl's flower girl dress from printed on the side of the package, and she grinned.

She picked up the box and brought it back inside the house.

"Guess what this is?" she said, shutting the front door and grinning at her daughter.

"Is it—?" Pearl clapped both her hands over her mouth.

"Your dress is here!" Caitlin shook the box excitedly, and Pearl leapt off the couch and raced toward her mother.

"Oh my goodness!" Pearl cried, bouncing up and down. "I can't wait!"

"You must be feeling better," Caitlin said, laughing, as she set the box down on a table by the window and started to open it.

"Oh, I am now," Pearl said. "The dress cured me."

Laughing, Caitlin finished opening the box and pulled out Pearl's dress. It was pink and frilly and charmingly designed. The little girl squealed as soon as she saw it.

"It's so pretty," she gasped. "Can I try it on right now?"

"Yes, you may!"

With another excited exclamation, Pearl grabbed the dress and took off. Caitlin arched a brow at her daughter as she took off running toward the bathroom, looking as though she was perfectly well. Chuckling, Caitlin began to tidy up the package materials—she broke down the box to be recycled and threw away the plastic bag that the dress had been wrapped in. By the time she was finished, Pearl had gotten changed into her flower girl dress, and her smile lit up her whole face.

"Look at me, Mommy!" the little girl cried, sashaying down the hallway. "Look at how beautiful my dress is." She paused and twirled, and the skirt of the dress rippled.

Caitlin felt tears spring into her eyes. Pearl looked beautiful, and Caitlin felt sentimental, thinking about her daughter walking down the aisle as a flower girl. It made the upcoming big day seem all the more real. It was such a huge moment in both of their lives, bringing Michael officially into their family. Caitlin was so happy that Pearl was just as excited to celebrate the marriage as she was.

"Come here, honey," she said, folding her daughter into a hug. "I'm so glad you like the dress."

"I love it. Thank you, Mom."

Caitlin could feel Pearl wiggling out of the hug, and she laughed and stepped back.

"You want to go look at it in the mirror?" Caitlin asked her. "The big one in my room?"

"Yes!" Pearl took off running down the hall, and Caitlin followed her, smiling and feeling her heart glow with happiness.

* * *

Gwen turned over in bed for what must have been the twentieth time. Outside, the wind was whistling against the eaves of the house, and she could hear an owl hooting in the distance. She felt as though she was living in the middle of the countryside, not tucked into the center of a town. It was late enough that she wasn't even hearing any cars drive past—only the sounds of nature.

She rolled over again and stared at the ceiling. The streetlamps outside were casting a faint glow across her apartment, and a tree was making shadows across her ceiling. She watched the shadows of the leaves flicker and dance, feeling just as restless as they looked.

"I give up," she murmured finally, sitting up and clambering out of bed. If she was awake, she might as well be doing things.

She padded into the kitchen in her slippers and began to make herself some tea. She poured a precise amount of water into her tea kettle, and then measured a teaspoon and a half of loose-leaf tea into her tea strainer, which was round and plain.

As she waited for the kettle to boil, she leaned against the counter with her arms crossed, staring into space.

She couldn't stop thinking about that man, that Isaiah Dunlap. He was so handsome, and he seemed roguish and full of life. She didn't know why she felt so drawn to him, especially considering how laid-back he was. He was the complete opposite of her in that way—she wanted everything to be done a certain way. She was surprised that she would be drawn to someone like that.

Especially after Ron, she thought, pressing her lips together.

Ron had looked like the put-together type—he dressed very smartly and he kept his appearance neat and professional-looking. At first, Gwen had thought he would be precise about details just like she was. When it had become clear how laid-back he was, at first, she'd told herself it didn't matter, and that their differences could work together. But Ron had become irritated with her habits—he hadn't liked how rigidly organized she was. He'd kept telling her that she needed to do things differently, and getting frustrated with her precision, calling her "uptight."

Ron had clearly not been the right guy for her. So now why was she feeling drawn to another man who was also clearly laid-back—seemingly even more laid-back than Ron was?

I can't help thinking that Isaiah is different, she thought, lifting the tea kettle off the stove as it began to whistle. *He seems laid-back, but he also seems very competent. He's smart, and it's clear that he knows how to work hard.*

She frowned as she poured hot water into a mug. Ron really hadn't been on top of things. Maybe someone who was laid-back wouldn't be bad for her as long as he was someone who understood what it was to have a strong work ethic.

She started to pace around her kitchen a little as she waited for her tea to steep—she checked the time, wanting it to steep for four minutes precisely. Outside, the same owl hooted again, and she frowned in surprise that she could hear owls even in town.

It just went to show what a sleepy little town it was, she thought. Even wild animals felt comfortable being there at night.

She checked the time and continued to pace. She found herself wondering if she would ever find someone who was a good match for her. She felt that she wouldn't be able to let go of her need for structure—she could never understand how other people could be so haphazard. Would she be able to find someone who was as careful about details as she was? She was beginning to think that was very unlikely.

By the time her tea was fully steeped, her mind was filled with questions about what a healthy relationship would look like for her. She took her mug and sat down at the kitchen table, drinking the hot liquid carefully.

Was there a middle ground? she wondered. Could she find someone who was willing to compromise, and accept the way she liked to do things? Could she compromise too, and learn to not care quite so much about how everything was done?

She took another sip of her tea, savoring the herbal flavor. Outside, the wind whistled against her apartment, rattling the windowpane a little bit. She heard a car passing on the street below, and she felt surprised—and, strangely, a little less lonely. It felt good to know that she wasn't the last person left awake in the whole town.

She sat quietly for a while, mulling over her thoughts. In the past, she'd never had a lot of time for just sitting and thinking. Her workload in New Hampshire has been so heavy that she'd been constantly going from working to running errands to working out to cooking to spending time with Ron to sleeping to working again. She'd managed to get it all done with a precision that was just shy of superhuman, but nevertheless it had been exhausting. Now that her workload was so much lighter in Blueberry Bay, she was finding that she had a lot of time on her hands, and she felt uncomfortable with it. She didn't know what to do with all that time —she wasn't used to just doing nothing. It was as if she was a machine that was always set to high power mode, and she was finding herself having to learn how to be in medium or even low power mode.

She felt uncomfortable with her new schedule. Her new, slower pace of life was giving her a lot of time to think. And meeting the residents of Blueberry Bay and seeing how they lived their lives was giving her a lot to think about. All of the people in town appeared to operate at the slower pace that she seemed to have been forced into—and they all seemed happier than the busy people in New Hampshire had been.

Could she really start a new life there in Blueberry Bay? She felt so different from all the people she'd met there. They were wonderful—she liked them a great deal—but she felt as if she was coming from another planet or something like that. The energy with which she lived her life was so different from theirs. She thought about Olivia, who had seemed so happy when she talked about her family and her boyfriend. She'd seemed like such a genuine, compassionate person. And then there was Caitlin, who had been so kind and sweet.

Gwen took another sip of tea, wondering if she

would ever be able to fit into Blueberry Bay. She tried to picture herself as a thriving member of the community, and she couldn't quite manage it. She had a feeling she would need to change before that could happen, and she didn't want to change.

She sat quietly for a while longer, slowly drinking her tea and at last feeling herself become sleepy. She stood up, rinsed out her cup, and set it inside the dishwasher. Then she crawled back into bed and shut her eyes, enjoying the feeling of the cool sheets against her cheek.

Would she ever fit into Blueberry Bay? she wondered as drowsiness swept over her.

And would she ever find the kind of person that she could build a life with?

CHAPTER ELEVEN

Isaiah whistled to himself as he walked along the sidewalk toward Gwen's private medical clinic. It had been several days since his injury, and he was on his way to get his stitches taken out. He was looking forward to getting them removed, and he was also looking forward to seeing Gwen again. He was curious to see if she'd warmed up to him at all since the last time he saw her.

He opened the front door of the clinic, and was greeted in a friendly manner by Heidi, who then led him back to the examination room. He sat down, waiting for Dr. Gwen to arrive and feeling a mixture of excited and slightly nervous.

She stepped inside the room, looking prettier than usual in mint green scrubs. Her cheeks were a little flushed, and the added color seemed to bring out the intensity of her eyes.

"How are you feeling?" she asked briskly, still maintaining her no-nonsense doctor's tone.

"I think I might live after all," he said, grinning at her. "How are you feeling?"

She gave him a polite smile, but he got the impression that she was trying not to laugh, and that delighted him. "I'm fine, thank you," she said primly, going to prepare her tools.

She removed his stitches in her quick, dexterous manner. "Keep your hand bandaged for a few more days, until the wound is fully healed. It's important to keep bacteria out." She continued to talk as she sanitized his hand and rebandaged it, giving him careful instructions on how to care for his healing cut. He heard everything she was saying, but he was finding it a little difficult to concentrate. He liked the precise, efficient way with which she spoke—he found it impressive that she was so good at her job.

"Anything else, Doctor?" he asked when she had finished bandaging his hand.

"Just don't intentionally impale yourself again," she said dryly, and he grinned.

"Yes, ma'am," he said, pleased by her quip and even more pleased about the way her eyes were twinkling. He could see a teasing glint in her eyes, and he liked it. "For your sake, I'll refrain from impaling myself."

"For my sake?" she countered, cocking her head. "What about for your own sake?"

"Oh no," he said, grinning. "Only for you."

He was allowing himself to be more flirtatious with her, leaning forward and maintaining eye contact with her. She smiled at him, a little coyly, and his chest filled with butterflies.

"I'll walk you out into the lobby," she said, hurrying over to the door as if she suddenly felt awkward.

He stood up and followed her, keeping his eyes fixed on the back of her head and trying not to grin too much. He wondered what was going through her mind.

As they stepped through the doorway into the lobby, he heard his sister Olivia's voice. His eyebrows lifted as he saw Olivia standing at the front desk, talking to Heidi.

"Isaiah!" Olivia said, feigning total surprise when she saw him. "What are the chances we'd be here at the same time?"

He had to suppress a laugh. His sister was pretending it was a huge coincidence that she was there at the same time that he had his appointment, but he knew it wasn't a coincidence—he'd told Olivia when his appointment was. After a second, he remembered that Olivia had made a point of asking him when his appointment was, so it was clear she had been scheming this moment for a while.

"Hey, sis," he said, giving her a hug. "I'd say the chances were pretty high," he added in a wry whisper.

Olivia smiled serenely as they separated, appearing unfazed that he had called her out on her shenanigans. "I'm here to bring some fresh basil from my house plant to Heidi and Gwen. That little guy is overflowing with leaves, I need help eating them all."

"Aww, thank you!" Heidi said, taking the bag that Olivia handed her. "I'll go put this in the fridge right now."

She ducked into the back room, and Olivia turned to Gwen with a smile.

"This one's for you," she said, handing her a sandwich bag stuffed with basil leaves. "They taste absolutely delicious on a caprese sandwich—I like to use fresh tomatoes from my aunt Marsha's garden. She's got plenty, I'm sure she'd be happy to give you some when they're grown. They're so much better than the ones from the store."

"I haven't met your aunt yet, I wouldn't want to impose," Gwen said, a little stiffly. "But thank you for the basil. This is very nice."

"Well, we should remedy that!" Olivia said with a guileless smile. Isaiah had to repress an urge to chuckle. "Aunt Marsha is the absolute best. She's planning on coming by and helping with some of the renovations for Little Clams. Oh!" Olivia placed her hand on her heart, clearly pretending to get an idea at that moment, and Isaiah lifted his eyebrows curiously, wondering what she was going to say. He knew his sister had some kind of scheme up her sleeve.

"I have a great idea," Olivia gushed. "What if you also help out with some of the renovations at the elementary school? After all, Isaiah needs some help now that he doesn't have full use of both hands."

Gwen's mouth had popped open in surprise, and Isaiah protested quickly. "Olivia," he said. "She's a doctor, and a very busy woman. She doesn't have time to help us renovate the school."

"Well, I'm actually not that busy," Gwen said, flushing a little, "but I don't know the first thing about renovating. I'd be absolutely useless to you."

"Oh, don't say that," Isaiah said, smiling at her.

"I'm sure you'd be great at it with a little instruction. I've seen how good you are with your hands."

"See? It's settled." Olivia nodded firmly. "Gwen thinks she has the time and Isaiah thinks she has the ability."

Isaiah felt sure that Gwen was going to say no to the proposition—she seemed as though she was very slowly warming up to him, but that hardly meant that she would be eager to be his renovation pupil. But the doctor seemed to be charmed by Olivia in spite of herself.

"I can donate a few hours out of my week to a good cause," Gwen said hesitantly. "I'd like to be of what use I can be here in Blueberry Bay. I'm used to working much more than I have been, and I've been feeling a little restless."

"That works out so well!" Olivia said grandly, clapping her hands together. "Thank you so much, Dr. Gwen. You're helping out a lot of kids."

"I'd be happy to," Gwen said, smiling a little less stiffly than usual.

"Come by the elementary school in the evening in a couple of days," Olivia told her. "We'll have projects for you to work on then."

"Sure." Gwen nodded, and Isaiah could practically see the wheels in her mind clicking and whirring—he felt sure she was a woman who never forgot any kind of engagement.

"Thank you again," Olivia said warmly, and left the clinic.

"Gwen, I'm sorry," Isaiah said, turning to the doctor with an apologetic grimace as soon as his sister was gone. "Olivia shouldn't have asked you to donate your time like that. I know she means well, and she's getting a bit worried about getting everything done in time for Kids' Fest, but—" His voice trailed off.

And she's trying to matchmake the two of us, he thought, and then he felt as though he might be blushing slightly.

"It's quite all right," Gwen said, smiling. "I can understand her being worried under the circumstances." She lifted one eyebrow, fixing him with a knowing look. "Although you told her not to worry, no doubt."

"You're correct! How did you know?" He grinned at her.

"You're so laid-back," she said, and they shared a chuckle. "And optimistic. I expect you tell everyone not to worry."

"Again, what are these psychic powers that you possess?"

She laughed. "And I mean it. I'm happy to help.

After all, didn't you suggest that I get to know the town so that I'll learn how to fit in better here? I can't guarantee that that will work for me, but I'll give it a go."

He grinned at her, feeling thrilled. "Sounds great." He couldn't take his eyes off her face for a few moments—he felt so excited that she wanted to become part of Blueberry Bay.

"Why are you grinning like that?" she asked, flushing slightly and looking to the side.

"I like that you're willing to give Blueberry Bay a try, instead of just sticking to your first impression of the town and never budging on it."

"Well, I'm here," she said, shrugging. "I should get to know the place I'm living in."

"I'm sure you'll fall in love with it," he said, cocking his head at her.

"I might," she blurted, and then she flushed again.

At that moment, Heidi came back to the front desk, smiling cheerfully. "All right, Isaiah, let's get you all checked out," she said, sitting down with a breezy attitude.

Isaiah smiled at Heidi and then glanced back toward Gwen—but she'd already disappeared.

CHAPTER TWELVE

Willis pushed open the door to Marsha's little cottage by the ocean, taking a deep breath of the familiar smell of her home. The scent of her house varied a little depending on what scented candles she'd been burning, but it always smelled fragrant with floral aromas. That afternoon it smelled like lavender and cedar.

He smiled, hearing the sound of Marsha laughing with someone else in the craft room at the back of her home. He knew that someone must be Johanna, since he'd recognized her car in the driveway. He strode down the hallway, eager to see his girlfriend and give her a kiss.

The door to the craft room was open, and he stepped through it, grinning at the two women who were seated across from each other at the craft table, sipping mugs of tea and laughing.

"Willis!" Marsha cried with enthusiasm when she saw him, and she stood up and hurried into his arms.

"I hope I'm not intruding," he said, planting a quick kiss on Marsha's mouth. "You ladies look busy."

"We're having another knitting lesson," Marsha informed him, giving his hand a squeeze before he drew back.

"But don't worry, we're almost done," Johanna said, looking up from the sweater she was knitting and grinning at him. "I'll leave you two lovebirds alone in a minute here."

"How are the lessons coming?" Willis asked, stepping over to the craft table, where Marsha's sweater was resting. It looked as though it was going to turn into an impressive work of art. Johanna's sweater, which she was holding in her hands, was made of a far simpler pattern but looked neat and professional.

"Amazing," Marsha said warmly. "Johanna is an excellent student."

"You know, a few months ago, I would never have agreed with that statement," Johanna said, taking a sip of her tea. "And I still think 'excellent' is much too hyperbolic, but I am proud of what I'm making here. I really have made improvements."

"Country living is growing on you, it seems," Marsha teased, her eyes gleaming with amusement. "Look at these country girl skills you're mastering."

Johanna chuckled. "Dating a fisherman will do that to you. I'm starting to feel like I grew up out here." Her eyes glowed when she talked about her boyfriend, Everett Howell.

"Wow, you've got it that bad, huh?" Willis teased. "Marsha, we need to do something for poor Johanna. Love is brainwashing her."

Johanna laughed. "Let it brainwash me. I can't believe that a few years ago, I thought I'd never want to move away from New York City."

The three friends continued to banter and chat for a while longer, and then Johanna swallowed the rest of her tea and stood up briskly.

"I should get going," she said, smiling. "I'm making dinner for that fisherman of mine tonight, and I want to make sure I get started on it now so that it's ready when he gets done with fishing."

Johanna said goodbye to Willis, and then Marsha walked her to the front door. Willis stood in the craft room for a moment, admiring the sweater that

Marsha was knitting and wondering if she was planning on giving it to him—it was dark green, his favorite color, and it looked as though it was going to be his size. He smiled, feeling a rush of fondness for her sweep through him.

When he heard the front door close, he turned and started walking down the hallway toward his girlfriend.

"Want some iced tea?" Marsha asked him, giving him another hug when they reached each other. "We can drink it out on the back porch and catch up about our days."

"Sounds great," he said. He loved their time sitting on the back porch together. They would sit and drink beverages and talk about everything that was on their minds. It was a time for them to be quiet together and become even closer as a couple.

A few minutes later, they were sitting next to each other on a couple of comfortable wicker chairs, holding hands and sipping the delicious iced tea that Marsha had made.

"How was your day, sweetheart?" she asked him warmly. "How's everything at The Crab?"

"Today went well," he said, smiling at her. "The Crab had a lot of customers, and no complaints. And!" He grinned when he remembered his news. "I talked to Hannah today. She and Luke are coming to visit for Caitlin's wedding. I can't wait to see them." His daughter, Hannah, and her boyfriend, Luke, were both away at college together, and he always looked forward to their visits.

"I can't wait to see them either," she said, clearly thrilled by the news. "I know she's been visiting as often as she can, but it never feels like quite enough. Do you think she'll visit a little more often after she graduates?"

"I do," he said, smiling and feeling a rush of nostalgia. He'd hoped that Hannah would move back to Blueberry Bay for good after graduating, but he knew she needed to do what was best for her and her music career. "I think she'll want to keep spreading her wings to pursue her music passion, but I hope she'll always come home whenever she can. I know she loves her roots here, and she's going to keep her hometown close to her heart."

"And *you* close to her heart," she said, squeezing his hand.

He cleared his throat, nodding.

"I used to think I would worry about her a great deal if she didn't come home after college," he said, looking out across the ocean, watching the way the golden sunlight was dancing on the water. "But I don't feel that way anymore. I love that she has someone who will be there for her. Luke is a great guy, and I trust him to look after her."

She nodded and smiled, and then she got quiet for a moment, looking out across the ocean. A light breeze, which smelled fragrantly of Marsha's budding flower garden, brushed against their faces.

"Penny for your thoughts?" he teased, lifting his brows at her when she turned in his direction.

"I was thinking about Isaiah," she said, smiling fondly as she spoke about her nephew. "I want him to find something like that—a relationship with someone who will really be there for him. I think he could use it. He's so charming and friendly, but I think he's a bit lonely deep down. And he's the kind of free spirit that would do well with someone to anchor him."

"Hmm." Willis nodded, grunting in agreement. He was fond of the young man, and he agreed with what Marsha was saying.

She sighed, smiling, and he squeezed her hand again.

"I'm sure everything will work out fine for Isaiah," she said, and he thought he saw her eyes dancing more than usual.

"I'm sure it will," he said, bumping her shoulder with his.

They sat there side by side, sipping their tea and watching the ocean waves until it was time to go inside to begin preparing dinner.

* * *

Gwen glanced up nervously at the big red brick building of Little Clams Elementary School. Her stomach was flopping as if she was a little kid on her first day of school—except it was clearly the wrong time of day for school, since the first traces of a vibrantly pink sunset could be seen along the horizon.

She was there to help out with the renovations, as she'd promised, and she wondered nervously if Isaiah was going to be there as well. She kept telling herself it was unlikely—and she couldn't decide if she wanted him to be there or not. She felt disappointed about the prospect of him not being there, and anxious about the idea of him working with her.

Just before she'd reached the front doors, one of them opened, and Olivia stepped out onto the sidewalk, grinning at her.

"Dr. Gwen! I'm so excited you're here. Thank you so much for agreeing to help out."

"Oh, of course," Gwen said, a little breathlessly.

She followed Olivia into the school and couldn't help but admire how clean and charming it was. It was an older building, but it was clear that it had been lovingly maintained for many years.

"Let me show you the rooms where we plan to do 'glow-ups,'" Olivia said, gesturing down the hallway. "Hopefully you will have a lot of fun working on this. I always find these kinds of projects very exciting."

Gwen smiled feebly. "I don't know that I'm going to be of much use."

"I'm sure you'll be a great help," Olivia reassured her. "Besides, any help you can give us is welcome. You're helping us get ahead."

Unless I break something and set them behind schedule, Gwen thought pessimistically, but she just smiled instead of responding to Olivia out loud.

Olivia proudly showed her the classrooms where they wanted to do some minor renovations, and Gwen felt touched by the way Olivia's eyes shone when she talked about the school. It was clear she loved it very much.

"Let me take you down to the teachers' lounge,"

Olivia said, grinning, after they'd looked at the classrooms. "We have a lot of the supplies for the rooms stored in there."

Olivia led her down a couple of hallways until they reached a charming little teachers' lounge, decorated mainly in lime green and pink.

"What's that?" Gwen asked, laughing a little as she saw a giant smiley face made out of M&M's lying on one of the tables.

"What on earth?" Olivia laughed, clearly surprised by it as well. "Oh, I know."

"What?" Gwen prompted, curious.

"That was definitely put there by Isaiah." Olivia gestured to the M&M smiley face. "He's the kind of guy who does things just for fun. He likes to spread joy. I think he left these here as a surprise for us, since he knew we'd be here." She picked up a couple of the brightly-colored candies and popped them into her mouth.

Gwen didn't quite know what to make of that, but she took a few of the M&M's anyway, being careful to take them from the end of the smile so she left the shape of it intact. She couldn't help smiling herself over the whole thing. It was sweet, pun unintended.

"Let's sit down in these armchairs and discuss

the plan," Olivia said, walking toward a collection of armchairs placed by a window. "Do you want some coffee? There's a Keurig over there on the counter." She gestured to where a couple of coffee makers were nestled amidst racks of colorful mugs.

"Sure." Gwen made herself a coffee at the Keurig as she and Olivia began to discuss the plans for the classrooms.

"Let's create a spreadsheet with the schedule for each project," Gwen said. "That way, if we start to fall behind, we'll know how many more volunteers we need to ask for based on the number of hours we've fallen behind."

Olivia's eyebrows lifted a little, but she smiled. "Okay! Sure. Sounds like a good idea to me. Very efficient."

Gwen smiled, but she felt a little twist in her stomach. Olivia's surprised reaction had made her feel as though she wouldn't ever fit into Blueberry Bay—to her, a spreadsheet was a simple matter of course, but Olivia seemed to think it was a little bit of overkill.

At that moment, Isaiah stepped through the doorway of the teachers' lounge, grinning like Tom Sawyer.

"Hey, ladies!" he said cheerfully. "Mind if I join the party?"

"Not at all," Olivia said, grinning back at him. "You already provided the snacks, didn't you?"

He bowed and went to make himself a cup of coffee. "I might possibly be guilty of that. What have you been talking about so far?"

Gwen felt her flutters of nervousness whirl like butterflies in her chest when she looked at him. It was ironic, she thought, that he gave off such a relaxed energy but he made her feel so jittery.

"Gwen here just suggested a spreadsheet for every project," Olivia said. "That way we can track how many hours we might get behind so we know how many more people to bring in if necessary."

Isaiah turned to Gwen with a smile. "A spreadsheet, huh? Sounds smart, but I don't expect we'll need to be so careful in this case. Right now, we're still ahead of schedule. I'm sure everything will work out just fine." He leaned against the counter, grinning cheerfully.

"We can't just rely on luck," Gwen protested, feeling a little frustrated that he was shooting her idea down so quickly. After all, they'd asked her to help out—this was how she knew how to be helpful.

"I think we should have a detailed plan to make sure we stay on track."

"I agree with Gwen," Olivia said, although Gwen suspected she might be trying to keep the peace more than she was actually in agreement with her. "Let's use spreadsheets. I'm grateful for any help you can give us, Gwen."

"Great." Gwen smiled briskly. "What else could I do to be of help?"

"Would you be willing to write up a little ad, asking for paint donations for the activity rooms? We thought that could be a fun way to keep costs low. We don't need any particular color—bright colors are best, but anything will do. And if someone doesn't have enough of one color to paint a whole room, that's okay—then we'll just paint all the walls different colors, which will be fun for the kids."

"Absolutely," Gwen said, finding the idea resourceful and charming. "I'd be happy to write up an ad for that."

"Perfect." Olivia smiled. "You and Isaiah are the perfect team for this project. With Isaiah's optimistic enthusiasm and your practicality, you'll have every base covered."

Gwen felt herself flushing a little at the suggestion that she and Isaiah would be a good team together. Her mind flashed back to the thoughts she'd had in her kitchen late at night, about whether or not she could be in a partnership with someone as laid-back as Isaiah. Not that working together and being in a partnership were even remotely the same thing, she thought hurriedly—but she couldn't help making the connection that if they worked well together in one dynamic, they might work well together in other dynamics as well.

She glanced at him and saw that he was flashing that radiant grin at her. She felt her stomach flutter, although she kept herself from looking away too quickly.

I had no idea what I was getting into when I agreed to help out at the school, she thought.

She had a feeling that she and Isaiah were both about to challenge each other's ways of doing things a great deal.

CHAPTER THIRTEEN

Caitlin hummed along to the radio as she drove along the coastline. Behind her in the back seat, Pearl was reading a book and swaying back and forth a little as if in excitement. Ever since her flower girl dress had arrived, Pearl had been the picture of health again, and Caitlin was relieved that she'd recovered from the flu so quickly.

"How's your book, honey?" she asked, smiling at her daughter.

Pearl looked up and grinned. "Amazing! There's all kinds of stuff about time travel. Right now they're in the eighteen hundreds on a pirate ship."

"Ooh, sounds exciting," Caitlin said, grinning.

"Are we there yet?"

"Not yet." Caitlin chuckled. "Just another fifteen minutes or so."

"Thank goodness we get to eat cake at the end of this," Pearl said. "This has been one of the longest car rides of my life."

Caitlin chuckled again. She and Pearl were on their way to Providence, to visit Paige at her baking school there. Paige had baked up a few different wedding cake flavor samples, so they were on their way to meet with her and try the cakes. Michael wasn't able to join them for their "girls' trip," as they'd decided to call it, but they were planning on bringing pieces of the cake samples back to him so that he could help Caitlin decide on the flavor.

It was a beautiful, sunny day, and Caitlin's spirits were light. Their route took them along the ocean, and as they drove they got to experience many breathtaking views of the blue water sparkling in the sunlight.

Finally, they arrived in Providence, and Pearl abandoned her book and glued her nose to the window, taking in the sights of the city with fascination. Before long, they arrived at Paige's charming apartment building, and she met them outside.

"So good to see you!" Caitlin said warmly, giving

the young woman a hug. "I can't wait to try what
you've made."

"I hope you like them," Paige said, smiling back
but holding her shoulders a little tensely as if she was
nervous. "I've got lemon, red velvet, chocolate
raspberry, and chocolate."

"Whoa," Pearl said, clearly in awe, and Paige and
Caitlin laughed.

Paige led them upstairs to her cozy studio
apartment, where she'd set out the various cake
samples on the counter.

"Paige, these are beautiful," Caitlin gushed,
looking in admiration at the miniature cakes that
Paige had frosted. "I didn't realize you were going to
decorate them too."

"Well, frosting plays such a huge role in the
overall taste of a cake," said Paige, smiling. She
seemed to be buzzing with a nervous energy,
although she was clearly flattered by the
compliment. "I wanted to make sure you got the full
force of every flavor."

"Please, can we try the chocolate one first?" Pearl
asked.

"Works for me," Paige replied with a nod.

"Please try the cakes with us," Caitlin said to

Paige. "I feel like you should get to eat some of your hard work."

"Sure." Paige smiled. "But only a little. I want to make sure we leave enough for Michael to try."

They began to sample the cakes, starting with the chocolate one, as Pearl had requested. As soon as Caitlin took her first bite of the rich, velvety taste, she was sold.

"Paige, this is absolutely incredible," she said, placing her hand on her heart. She stared down at the plate of cake almost in unbelief.

"It's amazing," Pearl agreed, talking with her mouth full of cake. "You should pick that one, Mom."

"Well, you should try them all," Paige said, looking very pleased.

"I'm excited to try the red velvet," Caitlin said.

The three of them continued to sample the cakes together, and Caitlin was thrilled that Josie had suggested Paige to her as a wedding cake baker. Even though Paige was young and still fairly inexperienced, it was clear that she more than made up for those things with her talent and her hard work.

After they'd sampled every flavor of cake, Caitlin was leaning toward the lemon and the red velvet—

although she also loved the chocolate, and she had a feeling that might be Michael's favorite.

"It'll take us a minute to make a decision," she said to Paige. "Michael will have to eat them, and—" She paused as she saw the young woman's shoulders droop. It was clear that Paige thought she was talking about whether or not to hire her for the wedding. "Oh, I just mean decide on what flavors, Paige! I'm so sorry, I should have made that clear. You're hired. Hands down. No questions."

"Really?" Paige asked, her eyes lighting up.

"Oh, absolutely," Caitlin said warmly. "These are amazing."

"Wonderful!" The young baker's cheeks were flushed, and she was grinning. "I'm thrilled. Just let me know what structure you want, and then we can talk about icing designs and any wedding cake toppers you might want. I'm learning how to make sugar sculptures, so that might be a fun option."

Caitlin's mouth dropped open a little. "Wow. That sounds incredible."

"Yay!" Paige, who had been acting carefully professional up until that point, seemed to burst out of her shell as her excitement won over. "Thank you!" she exclaimed, hugging Caitlin. "I absolutely cannot wait to make the cake for your wedding."

Caitlin nodded as they drew apart. "Of course. I love that I can support a young businesswoman. And in addition to hiring you to make the cake for our wedding, I'll make sure people know that you made it, so we can get the word out about your bakery even more. Everyone on the guest list will know about your bakery."

Paige flushed, pressing her hands to her mouth. "That would be amazing, thank you."

"I wouldn't think of passing by that opportunity to support you. You've been working so hard, and you have such a gift. We all want you to succeed."

Caitlin noticed Paige blinking back a few tears, so she tactfully hurried to change the subject.

"Let's all go out to dinner—my treat—and then we can come back here and pack these up to bring home to Michael."

"Sounds wonderful. And since it's not quite dinnertime yet, would you two like a little tour of Providence?"

Both Caitlin and Pearl agreed enthusiastically, and a few minutes later the three of them were stepping back out into the sunshine together.

CHAPTER FOURTEEN

Isaiah ran his fingers through his hair, taking a deep breath of the tangy, salty smell of the ocean. He smiled, feeling a wave of excitement. He was on the dock, getting ready to take the jet boat that he was renting for the duration of his visit out onto the water. He was looking forward to coasting along the waves and watching the sunset, which he expected to be breathtaking considering how nice the sunsets had been the last few days.

Just before he got into the boat, he caught sight of Gwen walking along the end of the dock. He froze the moment he saw her, finding that his heart was suddenly thumping. She had a stack of papers in her hand, and he realized that it was the fliers that she'd made for advertising about paint donations for Little

Clams. She must be in the middle of going around town, posting fliers, and her wanderings had led her down to the dock—to right where he was. All of a sudden, he felt extremely lucky.

"Gwen!" he called.

For a moment, she didn't seem to know where his voice was coming from—he guessed that the sound was being carried oddly because they were close to the water. She turned around in a circle, looking around for the person who had called her name, and then she caught sight of him. For a moment, she froze, and then she raised a hand in greeting.

Grinning, he began to hurry along the dock toward her. She approached him a little more slowly, with the fliers flapping in her hand and a polite smile on her face.

"Hey," he said, stopping when he was a few feet in front of her. "How's it going?"

"Good," she said, holding up the stack of fliers. "I've been wandering around town putting these up."

"I see that," he said, a grin tugging at his lips. "A carefree task looks good on you."

As soon as the words left his mouth, he wondered if she might get annoyed by them—he'd been pretty forward.

But she laughed and nodded. "It is kind of nice to do a task that doesn't involve a person's life or well-being. I'm used to there being a lot of pressure when it comes to work. This is a nice change." For a moment, the two of them stood there smiling at each other, and then she asked, "What brings you out here?"

He gestured with this chin back toward where his jet boat was bobbing in the water. "I'm about to go out on the ocean in that. Isn't she a beauty?" There was a short pause, and he watched her taking in the sight of the jet boat with a slight frown. "Have you ever been out in a jet boat?"

"Oh my goodness, no," she said, laughing breathlessly. "I've heard they're very dangerous. Can't people get flung off the side?"

He shook his head. "Lots of things are dangerous if you're not careful. If the weather is bad or if the person piloting the boat is inexperienced, it's possible for people to get flung off the side if the boat gets rocked too far one way or the other. And you want to stay away from the jet in the back, that's for sure. But those dangers are very rarely encountered. Not something a careful person like yourself needs to worry about."

"I don't know," she said. "Maybe a careful person

like me just wouldn't get on the boat in the first place." She returned his playful smile, and he chuckled.

"Can I have a chance to prove to you that the boat isn't as bad as you seem to think?" he asked. "It might even be a little bit of fun," he teased, wheedling a little.

She hesitated for a moment, biting her lip. "I shouldn't," she said, holding up her stack of fliers. He saw her glance nervously at the boat, making it clear that she still felt it would be unsafe to get on it.

He felt his stomach squirm—he didn't want to stop talking to her or hanging out with her. "Are you being a chicken? I dare you to come on the boat with me."

She rolled her eyes. "No wonder you work at an elementary school, you fit right in there."

He laughed, delighted by her teasing. "Okay." He shrugged. "I guess you're chicken."

She reached out and swatted his arm, and they both laughed. "Okay, fine," she said. "I'll get on the boat."

"Amazing," he said, feeling his heart do a couple of somersaults in his chest. "And rest assured, I'm very experienced with boats, and I'll be careful."

She nodded, still looking a little nervous, as they

walked down the dock to the boat. He got in first and then helped her get into it. She took a deep breath as she clambered on, looking nervous, and he gripped her hand firmly to reassure her.

"You're going to be just fine," he said, and she smiled at him, seeming to be steadied by his words. "You can sit right there," he said, gesturing to the seat placed alongside the pilot's chair. "And don't worry, there are lots of things to hold onto," he teased, and she stuck her tongue out at him.

Laughing, he sat down at the helm and started the engine. She tucked the fliers into her purse, which they stowed inside a compartment. Carefully, he pulled the boat away from the dock, glancing at Gwen to make sure that she wasn't feeling too nervous. She was holding tightly to the boat railing on one side and the edge of her seat on the other, but her eyes were bright with interest, and he smiled.

"Feels nice, doesn't it?" he said, as a gust of wind whipped their hair back. "I'm going to start giving it some speed, okay? Let me know if it's too much."

She nodded, and he accelerated the boat. It whipped across the waves, and he let out a whoop of excitement. He glanced over at Gwen, who was clutching her handholds and closing her eyes a little. After another second, she shrieked.

"Is that too much?" he shouted over the wind. "Do you want to stop?"

She hesitated for a moment and then shook her head, and he grinned, liking her bravery. He continued to steer the boat farther out into the ocean, feeling excited that she was there with him and wondering what adventures they were going to have together.

CHAPTER FIFTEEN

Gwen shut her eyes tightly, feeling the wind rush against her face. She hadn't expected being on the boat to feel so exhilarating—her heart was thumping, and she was feeling an adrenaline rush like she hadn't experienced in years. She felt terrified, but the good feelings she was experiencing were so intense that it was as if her fear didn't matter. She was strangely having the time of her life.

She loosened her grip on the chair and railing a little bit and opened her eyes slightly. The feelings of both fear and exhilaration rushed through her—it was a strange combination, but she liked it. It felt almost as if she was flying. As Isaiah accelerated the speed of the boat even more, she let out another shriek that sounded more like a whoop than the previous one had.

After another few minutes, he finally slowed down the jet boat. It began to coast slowly across the waves, and she opened her eyes fully, laughing breathlessly. She looked over at him and saw that he was grinning at her.

She took a deep breath, feeling her pulse start to slow down a little. She was grinning too—she couldn't seem to stop smiling. All of that adrenaline was still rushing around inside her, making her feel wild and alive.

"Well?" he said, cocking his head to one side. "What do you think?"

She took another deep breath, looking out across the ocean. The coast was a vision of green in the distance, and all around them sparkled vibrantly blue water. It was breathtaking, and she felt a leap of joy at the sight.

"It's extremely beautiful out here," she said, smiling at him.

He laughed. "I mean the boat. What do you think of the boat?"

She grinned. "It's actually pretty fun. I have to admit, I'm very surprised that I like it."

"Amazing." He stood up and came to sit next to

her on a bench seat placed close to her chair. "I'm glad you like it. Surprises are exciting."

"Oh, I don't like surprises, usually," she said, laughing breathlessly. Her heart was still thumping, although now that the boat had slowed down, everything around them felt calm and peaceful.

"Really?" he teased, pretending to be aghast. "How come?"

She shook her head. "Doctors learn to hate surprises. I find comfort in things being orderly and predictable. Scheduled." She smiled.

"How's that working out for you? That life with no surprises?" He was looking right into her eyes, and her stomach did a somersault.

"Pretty well, I'd say," she said. She pointed to his hand. "It looks great, doesn't it? I'm a good doctor. I'm great at my job. Orderliness is very important to me."

"You definitely are a good doctor," he said, sounding as though he meant it sincerely, although he had a slightly impish smile on his face. "A very good doctor. And thanks for stitching up my hand." Then his smile faded, and his expression became more serious. That made her heart start to thud all over again, almost as much as it had when the boat was going fast. "But what about in the rest of your life?" he asked softly.

Her lips parted, and for a minute she didn't quite know what to say. "You mean in my personal life?"

He nodded, his eyes on her face, smiling again.

"Well," she said, letting out a deep sigh, "my ex, Ron, kept telling me I was too inflexible. He always complained about how efficient I was about everything. I have my ways of doing things, because they're the best ways I've found. He didn't like how organized I am."

He listened to her compassionately, nodding as she spoke. "That sounds like a tough situation for you to be in. But maybe letting some surprises into your personal life wouldn't be a bad thing. It's never too late to try a new mindset and give things a chance. I mean, hey—you thought you hated boats, but yet here you are. Having fun, right?"

"You're right," she said, smiling softly at him. She felt grateful for his empathy and his kind words. What he said made a lot of sense—maybe she had been missing out on opportunities by sticking too closely to what she had already decided to do and how to do it.

For a while, they didn't talk very much. Isaiah sped

up the boat again for another few minutes, and both of them laughed and cheered over the thrill of the speed. Soon, glorious pinks and oranges began to fill the sky as the sun set, and he slowed the boat down again so that they could properly soak in the breathtaking view.

This is actually a lot of fun, she thought. *It's the first 'just for fun' thing I've done in a long time.*

She smiled, feeling as though a weight that she hadn't known she'd been carrying lifted from her shoulders a little. Beside her, Isaiah leaned back in his chair, watching the sky with a rapt expression on his face. He looked almost as though he'd never seen a sunset before, he seemed so happy.

Finally, the light around them began to fade, and he turned the boat around and brought it back to the dock. He tied it down, and then helped her out of it. She felt a twinge of reluctance for their adventure to end, and she realized it was the first time in a long time that she hadn't been thinking about her schedule or to-do list at all.

"Thank you for pushing me out of my comfort zone," she said, shaking his hand once they were both standing securely on the dock.

"Anytime," he said, grinning.

For a moment, they both hesitated, and then he said, "I'll see you around?"

"Yes, I'll see you at Little Clams again soon."

He nodded, still smiling. "Sounds great. See you soon."

He turned and started walking down the dock. She watched him for a brief moment, and then began to walk away in the opposite direction. The wind ruffled her hair, and she smiled to herself as she meandered down the dock. She was glad she'd run into him, and that he'd convinced her to get on the jet boat in spite of her fears. It had been an unexpected adventure, and a good experience. She felt grateful to Isaiah for showing her how much fun being on a boat could be.

She glanced over her shoulder as she walked, looking for him. He was striding along the dock, his hands in his pockets. She could hear him whistling faintly, and she chuckled.

As she made her way home, she kept thinking about him. He was a bit of a puzzle to her, but he was a nice puzzle. He made her feel comfortable and at ease in a way that no one ever had before.

CHAPTER SIXTEEN

Isaiah stood in the center of one of the classrooms at Little Clams, slowly turning around in a circle and gazing at the walls. It was one of the classrooms that Olivia wanted repainted and spruced up, and he was mentally going through a checklist of all the things he needed to do to the room.

Stacked around him on the floor were several cans of brightly colored paint—and that wasn't even their whole stock. Ever since Gwen had put up her fliers around town, they'd had paint donations come flooding in. Olivia had been thrilled about all of the different colors they'd received—lots of yellows and blues and greens. She'd been organizing them into color schemes, choosing which cans would be used in each room.

"Clear everything to the side, wash the walls, do a primer," he muttered, wishing he'd brought a notebook or something to write it all down in. It would have been nice to have a list of some kind, to help keep his head on straight.

At that moment, Gwen stepped through the doorway to the classroom, and his heart skipped a beat. For a split second, he just stared at her, and then he grinned.

"Hey! I wasn't expecting you to be here."

"I know I'm unannounced," she said. "Look at me, being spontaneous." They shared a grin. "I took an early lunch and I'd thought I'd come see if any of the paint donations had arrived yet."

"Oh, they sure have," he said, chuckling. He gestured to the several cans of paint that were stacked in the center of the room. "And that's just this room. We've got like five more piles like this one."

Her eyes widened. "Really? That's amazing!" She looked down at the paint cans, clearly impressed. "I'm shocked."

"You make a mean flier, Dr. Gwen." He winked.

She seemed to blush a little under his praise, and she waved her hand through the air, dismissing his words. "That's not my fliers, that's the people here.

That generosity was already waiting for an opportunity to help, I just happened to nudge it. But I'm still surprised by how quickly they sent the paint cans in."

"I'm not surprised at all in a small, friendly town like this," he said, grinning at her. "Just like you said, the generosity is already there. People here like to help each other out, and everyone here is invested in the school. Olivia said we even got a few brand-new gallons of paint donated."

"That's wonderful," she said, looking sincerely impressed. "And from the looks of this stack and what you've told me, we don't need any more paint? We've already got enough?"

"Oh, for sure," he said. "We're up to our ears in paint. We'll be able to donate some of this ourselves once the renovations are done."

"That's amazing," she said. "I would have expected this whole process to take so much longer."

"You see?" he teased. "Some things just can't be scheduled."

"Yes, but if we had gotten behind—oh, fine." She laughed.

"Wow, her mindset is changing already," he said, leaning against the wall and grinning. "That boat ride really did wonders for you, huh?"

She shook her head, laughing. "What boat ride? I don't know what you're talking about."

"You haven't been thinking about it, huh? I bet it's been sneaking into your dreams. I bet you even want to go out on a boat again sometime," he teased.

He remembered what a good time she'd had. He'd loved the way she'd whooped and grinned in excitement over the boat ride.

"I don't know. Was that an invitation?" she asked.

He lifted one shoulder, his lips curving upward. "It might be."

"Huh. Interesting," she said, tilting her head to one side coyly.

He realized that they were both flirting with each other, and his heart rate picked up. In that moment, it struck him that Olivia had been right—he was interested in Gwen romantically.

The revelation hit him like a sudden clap of thunder.

He wanted to show her how responsible he could be, so that she wouldn't just see him as someone who was too laid-back for her. And even more than that, he wanted to help loosen her up, and show her how much fun life could be if she would let it. He felt like he'd been doing a good job of that already by taking her out on the boat and showing her that sometimes, things outside her comfort zone could be wonderful.

Maybe, he thought, his heart thumping, *maybe although we're different, maybe we really do complement each other. Maybe she and I could really be a thing together. A great thing.*

He felt startled by the realization that he was starting to think about her in a truly romantic way. After all, he'd told his sister and his aunt Marsha that he wasn't looking for romantic love, and he'd meant it sincerely when he'd said it.

But now, standing there with Gwen, everything that he thought he knew didn't seem to apply anymore. She'd turned his emotions upside down, seemingly without even trying to. She was a surprise. A wonderful, thrilling surprise.

All of a sudden, he felt tongue-tied. He was spinning with the revelation that he liked her—he *like* liked her—and it made him feel awkward all of a sudden. He felt flushed and a little self-conscious.

"Yeah, absolutely, if you want to come out on the boat again, you're very welcome to," he said, feeling as though he had a sudden frog in his throat.

"Okay," she said, a little hesitantly. It was clear that she could tell that something about his demeanor had changed, and she was probably wondering why. He stuffed his hands in his pockets, realizing all at once that they were starting to get sweaty. "Sounds good. Maybe we could schedule the next boat ride?" she teased gently.

He smiled. "Sounds great. Let me know when you're free."

"I will." She smiled back. "Well, I'd better get going. Good luck with the painting. I'll help out with it the next time I come by to volunteer."

"You have to go?" he asked, unable to conceal his disappointment.

"Yeah, I do," she said. "I have an appointment in a little while so I should get back to the clinic."

For a moment she hesitated, her expression quizzical, as if she was about to ask him what was on his mind. But then she just smiled and turned around and left the room, waving goodbye as she went.

"See you later!" he called after her.

The moment she disappeared, he ran his hands through his hair. "Oh boy," he said, his heart pounding a little. For a few heartbeats he just stared at the empty doorway, feeling a rush of unexpected emotions.

Finally, he chuckled, shaking the feeling off.

Time to get back to work, Dunlap, he told

himself, squaring his shoulders and trying to force his mind back to the task at hand. *There will be plenty of time to think about this new revelation that you have a raging crush on the pretty new doctor. Right now, you need to focus on what you have to do.*

But he had a feeling that even while he continued to work, he was going to be thinking about her all day.

CHAPTER SEVENTEEN

Paige took a deep breath, standing at her baking station in one of her favorite classrooms. It was her very last class at Flourish Baking School, and her professor was walking from station to station, tasting everyone's final projects and explaining to the room what each student had done well and what needed to be improved on.

She glanced at the clock, her heart thumping in her chest. In just a few more minutes, she would be done with school. It was a bittersweet feeling—she'd loved her time at the baking school, and she'd made friends that she wanted to stay in touch with for the rest of her life—but her time at school ending meant that something new could begin. It meant that she could move back to Blueberry Bay and begin her own bakery.

This was always supposed to be a staircase, not a destination, she thought, looking around the classroom at her friends and feeling a rush of nostalgia. *And now I've climbed it, up to where I wanted to go.*

She had to suppress a smile, she suddenly felt so excited. Her professor stepped up to her baking station next, and sampled her final project, which was a lemon meringue pie decorated with miniature macarons.

"This is wonderful, Paige," her professor said warmly, and turned back to the whole classroom. "Paige mixed the meringue just the right amount for both kind of bakes. And her flavors are excellent."

Paige inhaled, feeling thrilled. Her professor continued to walk around the room, sampling bakes, for another few minutes. Finally, every station had been critiqued, and the professor stood at the front of the room, smiling at her students.

"Well, everyone, you did it. Congratulations. You've just finished baking school."

At that moment, the bell rang and the room erupted into cheers. Paige and her classmates hurried into a group hug, and for the next half hour, they talked and hung out and tried each other's final projects. Lots of people told Paige that her lemon meringue pie was the best one they'd ever had.

After they'd all finally spilled out of the classroom together, Paige wandered the school for a while, finding other classmates and professors that she wanted to say goodbye to. Finally, feeling full almost to bursting with a bittersweet ache, she made her way back to her studio apartment, which she'd already packed up for the most part. She put a few remaining items into boxes, finished cleaning, and then started to load up her car. Since it had been a furnished apartment, she didn't have to bring back any furniture, just her belongings, and the process didn't take as long as she'd expected it to. Soon she was standing in an empty apartment with a full heart, taking a deep breath and feeling ready to take the next step in her life.

She left her apartment for the last time, leaving her keys at the front desk. As she walked to her car, she glanced in the direction of Flourish Baking School, which she could partially see in the distance.

"Goodbye," she whispered, smiling quietly to herself. She took one more deep breath, and got into her car.

Blueberry Bay, here I come, she thought, and a grin spread over her face.

She made the drive back carefully but as quickly as she safely could. She couldn't wait to see Josie and be back in town. She'd been waiting for this moment for a very long time, and she was so excited to finally have made it that she felt a little bit as though she was dreaming.

At last, she pulled up in the parking lot of Josie and Wesley's apartment building. The plan was for her to stay with them for a few weeks until she found her own place in Blueberry Bay, and even though she didn't want to intrude on their newlywed life, she had a feeling the three of them were going to have a blast together.

The second she parked, she climbed out of her car and called Josie.

"Hey, sister!" Josie sounded beside herself with excitement. "When are you going to be here?"

Paige did her best to sound tired and disappointed, which was hard because she was practically squirming with happiness. "Hey, Josie, I got kind of delayed."

"Oh. Oh, well, that's okay." Josie sounded as though she was trying to hide disappointment. "I know you had a lot going on today. How much later do you think you'll be?"

"I think," Paige said, practically tiptoeing across the parking lot toward the front door of the building, "that it will be... as long as it takes you to come downstairs because I'm outside!"

"What?" Josie shrieked. "You—you—ahh!"

Paige laughed, and Josie hung up the phone. Less than a minute later, Josie burst out of the front door of the building and practically tackled her sister in a hug.

"I'm so happy to see you!" Josie cried, rocking her back and forth. "Congratulations on finishing baking school! I'm so proud of you."

"Thank you!" Paige grinned from ear to ear. "I'm so happy to be home."

"Come on upstairs and eat some dinner, and then we can all unload your car together. I made a white pizza with spinach. I know you love that."

"Oh my gosh, yay! But how did you time it out so perfectly?"

Josie laughed as they started upstairs together. "Oh, I didn't, I made it this afternoon. We just need to heat it up quick."

"Amazing." Paige's stomach grumbled in anticipation.

Wesley met them in the hallway and gave Paige a big hug. "Welcome home, Paige!"

"Thank you! Thanks for letting me crash your home."

"Hey, it was your home first."

"True!"

Paige and Wesley shared a grin.

"We've been so excited about you getting back," Josie admitted. "We've been planning your homecoming for a long time."

"We bought all your favorite snacks," Wesley said as they started toward the apartment door, which was ajar. "And Josie deep-cleaned your room and put like seven different scented candles in there."

"Wow." Paige grinned at them both, sighing happily. "It feels really good to be back."

Josie wrapped her arm around Paige's shoulders as they stepped inside the familiar apartment. It smelled incredible, like cooking food, and it soon became clear that Wesley had had the foresight to pop the pizza into the oven to warm as soon as Josie had gotten Paige's call.

"Look at these sisters," he joked, grinning at them as he shut the apartment door. "Reunited. A powerful force. I've just become superfluous, outnumbered by sisters. I am no longer needed."

They laughed at his joke, and Josie was quick to respond, "Oh yes, you are." She wrapped her arms around him, and Paige joined the group hug.

"We'll keep you around, Wesley," she teased. "Don't worry."

"Why thank you." He gave a small, exaggerated bow.

They ate a delicious meal of the white pizza with homemade French fries and a salad with blue cheese and black olives. As they ate, they caught up on each other's news, swapping stories and laughing together. Paige's chest glowed with a warm feeling, and she thoroughly enjoyed the meal, being very hungry from her long day.

When they were finished eating dinner, they went down to Paige's car and brought up her bags and boxes. With the three of them working together, the task took only a few minutes. They stacked everything in a corner of Paige's old room, and then Wesley volunteered to clean up the kitchen while Josie helped Paige unpack.

"Thanks, sweetheart," Josie said, giving him a quick peck on the lips as he was leaving. "I owe you one."

"No, you don't, it's my turn," he said, grinning at her, and disappeared.

"Wow, aren't you two adorably domestic?" Paige teased. "Taking turns doing the dishes, huh?"

Josie blushed, and Paige couldn't help laughing over how cute her sister was being.

"If that makes us adorably domestic, then I guess we're adorably domestic," Josie said, patting her cheeks. "We take turns cooking dinner and doing the dishes."

"Yup, definitely adorable."

They started to unpack Paige's belongings together, which were mostly clothes and books.

"How are you feeling about everything?" Josie asked, getting a tender tone in her voice which meant she was going into big-sister mode.

"Good," Paige said, smiling at her. "I mean, it's bittersweet for sure. I'm sad about saying goodbye to my friends, and I loved my time at school. And I loved that little apartment! But I'm so ready to be back here so I can start my next adventure."

"That's my girl!" Josie grinned at her. "And congrats on getting hired to make Caitlin and Michael's wedding cake. That's huge." Her eyes gleamed, as if she was proud of the hand she'd had in getting Paige hired.

"It is," Paige said. "I'm super excited about it. But I'm nervous too," she admitted, laughing breathlessly. "It's such a big deal, and I'm worried that something will go wrong. Caitlin is planning on telling everyone that I'm making her cake, which is so sweet of her, and it should help spread the word about my bakery business really well. But what if the cake doesn't turn out well, and then all those people think, 'Okay, let's not hire her'?"

"Paige." Josie looked her sister square in the eye. "Do you know how to bake?"

"What?" Paige stammered, confused by the question.

"Do you know how to bake?"

"Well, yeah, of course I do."

"Then bake the cake. Taste part of it to check the flavor and the consistency, and if you don't like it, make another one. But I know you. I know you're going to be careful and focused, and you're going to create an incredible cake that everyone is going to love to eat."

Paige let out a breath, feeling relieved by her sister's words. "You're right. I can do this. I made some pretty amazing wedding cakes in class."

"That's the spirit! Don't let your nerves get you down. You may not own an actual bakery yet, but you are absolutely a professional. And now you've got a diploma to prove it."

Paige scampered across the room and gave her sister a hug. "Thank you. I feel much less nervous already."

"Good," her sister said, grinning at her. "Now let's finish unpacking so we can watch a movie and eat the chocolate ice cream I bought."

"Ooh, really? That's an incentive if I ever heard one."

The two sisters continued to work, chatting about what movies they could watch. Paige felt tired but happy, and a feeling of peace washed over her. There might be challenges in front of her, but she trusted herself to accomplish them, and that was a good feeling.

* * *

Gwen rubbed her eyes, fighting back a yawn. It had been a long day at the clinic, and she was still there. She was just finishing up in her office, and she turned off her computer and carefully reset everything on the surface of her desk.

She stepped out into the lobby of the clinic, where Heidi was also getting ready to leave.

"I'm ready for a bubble bath and a glass of wine," Heidi commented. "Pink Moscato. It's been a long day."

"You're not kidding," Gwen said, smiling at her and feeling grateful that all she had to do to get home was climb a staircase. "Thanks for all your hard work today."

"You too! It was kind of nice to be so busy for a change—although I have to admit, I hope it doesn't stay this way all the time. I've been enjoying sitting here reading books in my downtime."

For a moment, Gwen didn't say anything. She was struck by the realization that she was starting to enjoy her new slower place of life a little bit as well. The revelation surprised her—had she really changed so much in such a short amount of time?

"Sounds like fun," she said, smiling at Heidi after a moment.

"What about you? You've been keeping busy with all this extra time we've had," Heidi said. "Are you still volunteering at the elementary school? Little Clams?"

"I am," Gwen said, feeling her heart lift up at the thought of it. "I'm going to go back there tomorrow morning to help Isaiah out with some painting. We're painting a lot of the classrooms in fresh colors, like green and blue. It's going to look really nice."

"You should ask him to take you out on that boat again after," Heidi said, grinning a touch slyly.

"What boat?" Gwen teased.

"Oh, I don't know, maybe the one you've been talking about almost nonstop ever since you went on it. Adrenaline suits you, Dr. Dunaway."

Gwen's mouth popped open—she was surprised by Heidi's comment. She had never considered herself to be the kind of person who was suited to adrenaline. "I don't know about that."

"Hmm, so maybe it's not the boat you're so excited about." Now Heidi's smile was decidedly sly. "Maybe it's the captain of the boat."

"What?" Gwen protested, feeling herself flush.

"Isaiah Dunlap, the heartthrob of Blueberry Bay. You've been spending a lot of time with him, and I'm not going to lie, you seem much happier than usual. So come on—you should ask him to take you out on that boat again. Maybe it will be like a date."

"I—no—I'm not interested in him like that," Gwen stammered. "I'm not going to ask him to take me out on the boat again."

The nurse lifted her eyebrows and cocked her head to one side, giving Gwen a skeptical look.

"What?" Gwen protested. "What's that look for?"

"It means that what you think of him is written all over your face," Heidi said, grinning. "You like him, and you want to get on board with his optimistic, fun-loving ways even if it is against your nature."

Gwen's mouth popped open again, ready to protest, but the words died on her lips. She couldn't deny it—she did find Isaiah fun and attractive and a great person to be around. She got butterflies whenever she thought about him, and that made her nervous. And she had to admit that she was now more nervous about the whole thing than ever before, since he'd acted a little strangely the last time she'd spoken with him. She'd been noticing the budding chemistry between the two of them, but the way he'd been acting the last time she saw him made her wonder if maybe he'd decided that they weren't compatible after all, and he needed to stop being flirtatious with her.

I scare people off, she thought. *No man wants to be with someone who's as particular as I am.*

Shaking off her disappointment at the thought, she said firmly, "I didn't come here to get into a relationship. I mean, I just got out of one. That's not part of the plan for me."

Heidi smiled knowingly, resting a hand on her hip. "Hey, sometimes things don't go according to plan. Sometimes you need to embrace the unexpected."

Gwen smiled back, but she didn't comment on Heidi's words. Internally, she knew that what her friend was saying made a lot of sense, but she didn't feel ready to admit that out loud.

"You keep thinking about it," Heidi said breezily, lifting a brow at Gwen and grabbing her purse. She seemed to sense that the conversation wasn't going to go anywhere else that night, but Gwen got the impression that her friend planned on bringing the whole thing up again another time. "I'll see you soon. You can tell me all about how the painting goes tomorrow."

"I'm sure it'll be fairly uneventful," Gwen said. "Paint drying is supposed to be one of the most boring things to watch, isn't it?"

"Yeah, but you won't be watching the paint dry," Heidi said mischievously. "See you tomorrow!" she called out cheerfully before Gwen had a chance to protest, and slipped through the front door.

Gwen watched her go, feeling her stomach fill

with butterflies. She was excited to see Isaiah the next morning, and she was nervous too. Part of her wanted nothing special at all to happen the next day, because that would mean that she could start to forget all about her crush on him and try to focus on other things. But the rest of her hoped that she would have news to share with Heidi after all.

CHAPTER EIGHTEEN

Alissa pushed open the front doors of Sandy's Grocery and stepped inside the cool store, taking a deep breath of the smells of bakery and produce. She'd been driving home after working at *The Outlet* all day when she'd suddenly felt overwhelmed by a craving for garlic bread.

Pregnancy is wild, she thought, adjusting her glasses with a wry smile as she made her way down the familiar aisles of Blueberry Bay's grocery store. *One minute I'm driving along deciding that Dane and I should just eat leftovers for dinner, and the next moment, I'm like a wild woman for a specific kind of food.*

She decided that she wanted to make fresh garlic bread, using a loaf of French bread from the bakery.

She got a shopping basket and began to make her selections, feeling excited about getting to enjoy the garlic bread when she got home.

She smiled as she approached the register, happy to see that her friend Sandy was working the check-out line.

"Sandy!" she said warmly as she started to unload her items onto the conveyer belt. "How are you?"

"Oh my goodness, Alissa! Let me give you a hug." Sandy stepped over to where Alissa was for a moment to give her a quick embrace. "How excited are you for the baby to arrive?"

"Practically beside myself," Alissa admitted, laughing. She could feel that her cheeks were flushed and her eyes were shining. "I'm so jittery and nervous, but I couldn't want anything more than I want Oscar to be born."

"I know the feeling," Sandy said, her eyes shining. Sandy had recently had a baby as well, and Alissa knew she understood what she was experiencing.

"I know you do," Alissa said. "Speaking of, how is Chandler doing?"

"Amazing," Sandy said. "He's the sweetest baby,

and not fussy at all most of the time. I think his big brother's calm energy rubs off on him."

Alissa grinned. Just before Chandler had been born, Sandy and her husband Daniel had adopted a teenager that they'd been fostering. Tommy was an outstanding young man—helpful, kind, and hardworking. "I can imagine those two men of yours are a lot of help," she said. "I'm so glad you have that support system."

"I am too. I'm so lucky," Sandy said. "And it's so sweet to be a family together. Most nights after Chandler's gone to sleep, we play board games or watch a movie. And Tommy's been learning how to cook, which has been such a godsend. He keeps making these amazing pizzas and pastas. It's like living in Italy—well, a teenage version of Italy."

Alissa laughed. "That's great."

"Speaking of meals, we're definitely going to make you some when Oscar is born," Sandy said. "Maybe Tommy will make this baked cheesy chicken alfredo that he's invented for you. I'll have to ask him if he will—it's so delicious."

"Ooh, that sounds incredible. Thanks, Sandy."

"Of course! I can't wait to meet your baby. A whole new Taylor. He's going to light up your world."

"I know he is." Alissa clasped her hands. "Got any advice for me?"

"Oh, absolutely." Sandy's eyes took on a faraway look for a moment, as if she was remembering the days when Chandler had first been born. "Give yourself grace, that's for sure. You don't have to do everything perfectly to still be a good parent. And expect to be tired, but try to maintain a positive attitude. Staying positive will make everything easier in the long run. And try not to be nervous," she added with a laugh. "I know it's hard, but it'll all work out okay. Lean on Dane when you're feeling jittery."

"I'll try." Alissa laughed. "But we've been trading off being the nervous one. If I'm nervous, he reassures me, and then if he's getting nervous, I reassure him."

Sandy laughed too. "That sounds like me and Daniel. We kept switching between reassuring and needing to be reassured."

For a moment, the two women smiled at each other, and then Alissa felt the baby kick in her stomach.

"Well, hey, you," she said, looking down at her stomach and talking to Oscar. "You want to say hi to Sandy?" She looked up and grinned. "He's kicking."

"Oh!" Sandy placed a hand on her heart, delighted. "It's such a wonderful feeling, isn't it? Like he's saying hello."

The two women continued to chat for a while longer, and the subject of Caitlin's wedding came up.

"I'm so excited about it," Sandy said. "I love weddings. I'm practically counting the days at this point—just a few more weeks!"

"I know! I'm so excited too."

"It's not too overwhelming, is it? With so much happening at once?"

"Oh, not at all. I've been helping Caitlin when I can, but she's such a powerhouse of efficiency that she hardly needs me! The most challenging thing has been shopping for a dress when I keep expanding," Alissa joked, grinning. "I'm having trouble finding a dress that's flattering and also big enough to accommodate me and the baby."

"With your pregnancy glow, you'd be gorgeous in anything," Sandy reassured her. "I'm sure you'll find something you love."

"Thanks." Alissa smiled, grateful for the compliment.

At that moment, someone stepped up in line behind her, so she paid for her items and said an affectionate goodbye to Sandy. As she was walking back out to her car, thinking excitedly about the garlic bread she was going to make, Oscar kicked in her stomach again.

She smiled and rubbed her belly fondly, looking forward to his arrival. Her conversation with Sandy had been encouraging, and she felt much less worried about everything. She got into her car and made her way home, feeling lighthearted and filled with hope for the future.

Isaiah took a deep breath, staring out the window of his short-term apartment. It was a beautiful evening, and he had every window in his place open, allowing in a refreshing breeze from the sea. Outside it was balmy and serene—which was the opposite of how he felt.

I don't know what happened to me, he thought, resuming the pacing that he'd been doing for the past twenty or so minutes. *It's like all of my chill has evaporated.*

But he did know what had happened to him— Gwen had happened to him. Ever since he'd realized that he was developing feelings for her, his easygoing coolness had floated out the window as easily as the spring breezes. He felt indecisive, nervous, and restless. He wanted to ask her out, but he wasn't sure if he should or not. He didn't know how she felt about him, and he didn't know if she might want more time before starting another relationship, since her last one had ended not that long ago.

He pulled his phone out of his pocket and stared at it as he continued to pace. He kept having the impulse to text her, but then he kept talking himself out of doing it. He didn't want to just ask her out over text out of the blue, but he was itching to have a conversation with her. He kept wondering what she was doing, and how her day had been.

Then he had an idea, and he grinned a little to himself. He paused in his pacing and sent her a text.

ISAIAH: Hey! Are we still on for painting tomorrow morning?

"This is good," he muttered. "She likes scheduling. She'll like that I'm thinking about scheduling too." Then he groaned, realizing how much he sounded like a lovesick puppy.

He took a few more steps, continuing to pace, and then his phone buzzed. Delighted and surprised, he checked the screen and saw that Gwen had sent an almost immediate response.

GWEN: We're still on. Why? Are you getting chicken?

He grinned, chuckling to himself, and texted her back quickly.

ISAIAH: Gosh, no. I'm an excellent painter. You should be feeling nervous, because you're about to lose tomorrow's painting competition.

In only a few more seconds, his phone buzzed with another reply.

GWEN: You might be good, but you're not better than me. I'm efficiency incarnate.

He laughed, finding that he was grinning from ear to ear like a goof. He hadn't expected her to be so funny, and he couldn't stop chuckling as they continued to banter back and forth over texting.

Finally, he took a deep breath, deciding that now was the moment—now before he lost his nerve. He carefully typed out his next text.

ISAIAH: Would you be up for another jet boat ride with me, even after a long day of painting?

He waited, no longer pacing, staring at the screen as he waited for her response. He hadn't made it entirely obvious that he was asking her out, but considering the flirtatious energy that had been happening between them, he felt as if she must have some inkling that he liked her. What if she read his invitation, and told him no? Wouldn't that imply that she was telling him she wasn't interested in him like that?

He swallowed, feeling his blood rush in his veins. He started to pace again, telling himself to take it easy, but he felt nervous as he waited for her to reply. Finally, almost five minutes later, his phone buzzed.

GWEN: Sounds great to me.

His eyebrows lifted, and the goofy grin returned to his face. He felt a rush of surprise that she'd said yes—he'd been telling himself that she was going to turn him down. He let out a huge sigh, his heart thumping.

All of a sudden, he couldn't wait for tomorrow.

CHAPTER NINETEEN

Gwen smoothed down her hair as she walked up to the front entrance to Little Clams. It was a beautiful Saturday morning, and although she felt a little jittery, her spirits were high. She was excited to spend the day painting, something she enjoyed, and even more than that, she was looking forward to going out on the boat with Isaiah when their work was done. She'd been thrilled when he'd started texting her the night before, and even though she'd had to wrestle with herself before agreeing to go out on the boat with him again, by that time she was feeling great about her decision.

She stepped inside the cool, dim building and began to make her way toward the classroom where she knew they were planning to start painting. As she turned down one of the hallways, she froze.

"What on earth?" she muttered, staring at the line of paint cans that was stretched along the wall.

She continued to walk, her confusion growing as the line of paint cans just kept going. She followed it all the way to the classroom where she was planning on meeting Isaiah.

He was already inside, whistling as he scrubbed the walls of the room, preparing them to be painted. He appeared perfectly calm and cheerful, something she couldn't understand considering the army of unwanted paint cans that was marching down the hallway.

"Good morning!" he said, his face lighting up into a grin when he saw her. "How are you this morning?"

"Confused," she said honestly. "What on earth is all the paint for?"

He laughed. "Well, we asked people to donate it, didn't we?"

"But—" She shook her head, feeling a wave of frustration over how inefficient their plan had turned out to be. This was why she always liked to plan things carefully! Because otherwise, things like this could go wrong. She should have thought more carefully about the whole situation once she'd realized how much paint was being donated. "This is too much. It's extremely inefficient. What are we going to do with all this extra paint?"

He shrugged, grinning at her. "We'll think of something."

"But—in the meantime, there's paint cans all over the school! Those will have to be cleared out, and we need somewhere to store them before we can find somewhere to donate them, if anyone could even possibly want that much paint—"

"Well, we do. We want lots of paint."

"Not this much!"

"Hey," he said, smiling at her reassuringly. "It's okay. The townspeople have been really generous. That's still a good thing! They're being supportive of the kids, and I think it's sweet."

Gwen opened her mouth to reply, but at that moment, someone stepped through the classroom doorway behind them.

"Knock knock," said a smiling man with a shaved head and a dark brown beard. "I'm here to make a paint donation." He held up a can of paint that had a splash of yellow painted on the lid.

Isaiah grinned gleefully, clearly amused by the way Gwen was trying to repress a groan.

"That's awesome, thank you so much, Daniel," Isaiah said, striding forward to take the can of paint and shake the man's hand. "We appreciate you helping out the school like this. Gwen, this is Daniel Ryan, who co-owns Sandy's Grocery with his wife. Daniel, this is Dr. Gwen Dunaway."

"I've heard great things about you and your practice," Daniel said, shaking her hand.

"Thank you," she said, feeling pleased by his words—but her feathers were still ruffled about the paint situation. "And thank you for donating," she added, forcing herself to say it.

"Of course! I want to make sure you have all you need to make the elementary school great for the kids."

She smiled a bit awkwardly, still feeling a little thrown by the whole situation and not knowing what to say in response to him. Out of the corner of her eye, she could see Isaiah grinning from ear to ear, barely able to hold in his laughter.

"Well, I won't keep you," said Daniel, smiling warmly at them both. "Best of luck with painting."

"Thanks, Daniel! Appreciate you!" Isaiah called, waving to the other man as he left the room.

The second he was gone, Isaiah doubled over with silent laughter. Gwen hid a smile of her own,

unable to keep from finding the situation amusing—
and the way Isaiah was laughing gleefully like Peter
Pan was endearing.

"You should have seen your face," he said at last,
wiping away tears. "Oh boy."

She shook her head, chuckling a little. "I have no
idea what to do with this. I might have made a plan
for what to do with this many paint cans if I'd had
any inkling things could have turned out this way.
I'm not used to people being overly generous. In my
experience, it's usually the opposite."

He grinned at her, gesturing around them. "I
know it seems like way too much, but we can sort
through everything later. This is a good thing in the
long run, because it opens up so many possibilities
for the classrooms. This way we can choose whatever
colors we want from our vast resources, and we can
even spruce up areas that weren't on Olivia's original
list. Remember that room we'd decided to give that
burnt orange accent wall, and we all thought it was a
little too dark for a kid's classroom? Well, now we get
to paint it a mint green, thanks to these new
donations."

She found her smile widening as she listened to
his words. Not only was she encouraged by what he
was saying, but she couldn't help being delighted by

the way he was so focused on good things, instead of letting himself get frustrated by their problems. She found herself admiring his positive attitude.

"How do you always manage to focus on the best scenario?" she asked. "You're so optimistic. It blows my mind."

"Oh, I wouldn't say always," he said, his expression shifting suddenly into a slightly nervous one. "I don't always focus on the best scenario."

She looked at the tips of his ears curiously—they seemed to be slightly pink. "What do you mean?"

"Well, like last night," he said, laughing breathlessly. "I wasn't feeling optimistic at all. After I asked you out, I kept telling myself you were going to turn me down. All I could think about was how nervous I was that you were going to say no."

Her heart skipped a beat, and her eyebrows lifted in surprise. "Oh. Well... um. Last night I kept telling myself you weren't really asking me out a date, and it was just a friendly boat ride."

"Oh," he said, his shoulders drooping visibly. "You—oh."

For a few seconds, they stood there staring at each other and neither one of them spoke. She felt breathless all of a sudden, and she had to make an effort to get her next words out.

"Because I was also feeling pessimistic and I didn't want to get my hopes up too much," she said, smiling shyly at him. "So you were asking me out? Like it's a date?"

"Yeah," he said, looking her right in the eyes and swallowing. "I really like you, Gwen."

"Okay." Her heart was hammering, and she had a tingling feeling all over her, like her blood was suddenly rushing faster. "Then yes."

"Yes? Yes, it's a date? That's what you want?"

She swallowed, and then she smiled. "Yes. Yes, it is."

He grinned, looking relieved. "Well, okay then." He let out a laugh, which she found adorable. "Great. A date it is."

She smiled at him, feeling butterflies dance in her stomach. She felt dazed. She'd had a moment of wondering if he'd been asking her out when they were texting, but she'd quickly told herself not to be silly and that he was just being friendly. The revelation that he had been asking her out—and he'd been so nervous to do it—made her feel as if she was suddenly walking on the clouds.

"We should get to work," she said, feeling as though she might be blushing and wanting to distract herself a little. "Are those the right cans of paint over there?"

"Wow, right to the grindstone, huh?" he teased, his lips curving upward.

"Well, we're here to paint, aren't we?" she said, unable to keep from smiling at him despite the way she felt flustered. "I want to make sure I'm doing my job."

"I think part of our to-do list can be getting to enjoy each other's company," he said, almost shyly. "After all, you're a volunteer. You don't have to take our tasks all that seriously."

"Mm, clearly you don't know me that well yet." She laughed, opening a can of paint and starting to mix it carefully.

"Well, I'd like to." He smiled at her, and she felt butterflies dance in her chest.

They began to paint the walls of the classroom a beautiful sunshine yellow. She enjoyed the work—the way they were transforming the room felt satisfying and almost exciting. And she was enjoying getting to work alongside Isaiah—she admired the way he moved quickly but not sloppily. He seemed to be focused on his work, and he hadn't been lying about the fact that he was very good at painting. Since she was as well, it was clear that they were going to complete each room they worked on together in excellent time.

She couldn't stop herself from glancing over at him now and again as they continued to paint. They kept bantering and teasing each other on and off, but even when they weren't having a conversation, she felt drawn to look at him. She felt curious about him in a way that excited her. She found herself wondering all kinds of things about him, and looking forward to having her questions answered.

She thought about her conversation with Heidi, about embracing the unexpected. She hadn't planned on becoming interested in someone romantically when she moved to Blueberry Bay, but it was certainly happening.

He's so good-looking, she thought, glancing at him again and biting her lip. *And more than that, he seems like such a good person. He's challenging me to see the world in a new way.*

She told herself that she was definitely going to have to learn to embrace the unexpected, since she was discovering that the unexpected could be wonderful. She couldn't think of anything that was more unexpected than this man stealing her heart and showing her how to think about life differently.

CHAPTER TWENTY

Isaiah glanced over at Gwen, feeling his heart thump with excitement. They were walking along the dock together toward his rented jet boat, and he couldn't believe she was really there with him and that they were about to go on an official date. He felt as though he should pinch himself to make sure he wasn't dreaming.

They'd spent a fun, rewarding day painting the school together. He'd been impressed by her work ethic and efficiency—her can-do attitude hadn't wavered once during the day even though they'd worked for a long time. They'd accomplished a great deal, and he guessed she felt just as proud of their work as he did.

"Are you excited?" He grinned at her as they reached the boat.

She nodded, looked flushed and a little nervous. "I am," she said, although she was looking at the boat as if it was a giant dog that she liked but thought might bite her.

He clambered on board first and then helped her onto the boat. She took her seat next to his pilot's chair, and as he started the engine of the boat, he glanced over at her. He saw her take a deep breath, looking out across the ocean with shining eyes. All of a sudden, he felt like he'd been hit in the stomach, she looked so beautiful.

"Are you ready?" he asked, grinning at her.

"Yes," she said without hesitation, although she gripped the handholds she'd used the last time.

He steered the boat away from the dock and then accelerated the engine. The boat zipped across the water, and he let out a whoop, thrilled by the speed. Wind whipped their hair back and a mist of salty water brushed their cheeks. He looked over at Gwen and saw that she seemed to feel more confident than she had the first time on the boat—she was leaning forward a little and smiling with her eyes wide open. He grinned, pleased that she seemed to be having a good time.

After enjoying the speed of the boat for a while, he slowed it down in a place where they had a breathtaking view of the ocean on one side and the coast of Blueberry Bay on the other. The sun was setting, and the sky glowed with pastel colors—pink and yellow and orange. A light breeze, scented with the salty smell of the ocean, kissed their faces.

"This is nice," she said, smiling and gazing out across the water at the incredible view. She turned to him, and her eyes had a glow to them. "I'm glad you invited me out here."

"I'm glad you came with me." He smiled back at her, feeling his heart dance with a rhythm similar to that of the waves rocking the boat underneath them. "I know you just got out of a relationship, so I appreciate you being willing to take a chance on me like this."

She nodded, keeping her eyes down shyly for a moment. "It's been a long time since I've been on a first date. But I—well, I wanted to be here." She looked up and smiled at him.

He grinned, feeling thrilled by her words. "It's been a long time since I went on a first date too," he said. "I kind of gave up on dating for a while there."

"How come?" She placed her hands in her pockets and leaned back in her chair as if she was settling in for story time. The gesture made him chuckle.

"Oh, well, I just never seemed to find anyone that I felt I wanted to make the effort for. I think my easygoing, casual nature kept me from getting serious about anyone. Pursuing a serious relationship always seemed like so much work and pressure, and I never felt the need to get into all that."

"Huh," she said, and for a moment he wondered what she thought of him.

"It's not that I don't want a serious relationship," he added hurriedly, "or at least—I always knew I wanted one eventually. But I'd wanted to keep things simple, not realizing that there's a lot of good things that are more complicated. Like relationships."

She nodded, looking out across the water but smiling a little at his words. "A lot of good things are very complicated," she said softly.

"What about you?" he prompted when she turned back to face him. "What's your story?"

"Oh, I don't know." She let out a long sigh and sat quietly for a moment, thinking. "I think I took my ex's words too much to heart. He told me that the way I was so inflexible made me impossible to deal with, and it was all too much, etcetera, etcetera. But I think I became that way in our relationship because he was so irresponsible. I overcompensated. He made me feel stressed out by how he lived and how little he cared about details, and it made me try that much harder to keep things in line in order to feel like everything was going all right. And who knows—maybe I could see that the relationship just wasn't working, and unconsciously I thought that fixing all the little details would fix the relationship itself."

He watched her, feeling his heart stir with compassion for her.

"I'm sorry you went through that," he told her.

She smiled at him. "It's all right. I'm learning better now. I'm feeling like I don't have to be responsible and rigid all the time, and that's been nice. The truth is that there's room in me to have fun and still take things seriously."

He nodded, feeling that her words applied to him as well. "Absolutely. Just like there's room for me to take things seriously and still have fun."

He waggled his eyebrows at her, then pretended to fall off the pilot's chair.

"See?" he said, lying on the bottom of the boat and grinning up at her. "I never would have done that if the boat was moving. I take safety seriously, but there's still plenty of opportunity to be silly."

She chuckled, reaching down to help him back up.

"You are a very silly man," she told him, pretending to scold.

"You're welcome," he said cheerfully, taking his seat again. "I made you laugh, didn't I?"

"Yes, you certainly did. You make me laugh a lot. I like it."

He felt his stomach warm with happiness. "I didn't see this coming, but I like it. I mean us. You make me want to make you laugh."

"I feel the same way. I didn't see this coming, but I'm glad it's happening."

For a moment, they smiled at each other. The wind rocked the boat gently back and forth and it bobbed up and down on the waves. The sunset shifted in its magnificent colors, allowing more deep blue to spread across the eastern edge of the sky.

His mind traced over the events of the past few weeks, wondering how he'd ended up sitting there across from her on a date. He started to laugh, thinking about the conversation that he'd had with Olivia.

"What?" she prompted curiously, her mouth curving up into a smile.

He shook his head. "Olivia. She predicted all

this. She was right about you and me becoming interested in each other—and I'd told her she was wrong and that I wasn't looking for a relationship and that was that, and now—well, now she'll never let me live it down."

"I'm sorry to hear that," she teased. "That sounds rough."

He laughed, enjoying her teasing. "It's totally worth it, though. I'm so glad I met you."

Her eyes seemed to glow a little more. "I'm so glad I met you," she said softly. Her shoulders were turned toward him, and her hands were clasped in her lap.

"Can I kiss you?" he asked, his heart hammering in his chest all of a sudden.

She nodded, looking a little wide-eyed. "Yes, I would like that very much."

He leaned in toward her, tucking a few strands of hair behind her ear. The whole world seemed to stop for a moment as he placed his lips gently on hers.

She gazed up at him as they pulled away from the kiss, her eyes shining.

"What are you thinking?" he asked, grinning at her.

"I'm thinking that was an amazing kiss," she said,

blushing a little, "and that I definitely have something to tell Heidi tomorrow."

He laughed, brushing his fingertips over her cheek again. His heart felt light and his stomach was fluttering with happiness. It had been an amazing kiss, and he felt excited about continuing to talk with her for the rest of their time out on the boat.

"Heidi's also matchmaking us, huh?" he asked, lifting a brow.

"I think so." She laughed too. "I think she got suspicious when I kept talking about our first boat ride almost nonstop."

"You did?" His lips curved up on one side. "That's awesome. You really liked it that much?"

"I really did." She glanced around at the water surrounding them. "And I like it even better today."

"Well, in that case—you want to go fast again?"

"Yes, please!"

He grinned at her and accelerated the engine, steering the boat out across the sunset-painted waves.

CHAPTER TWENTY-ONE

Olivia skipped up the front steps of her aunt Marsha's cottage, taking deep breaths of the wonderful smell of her aunt's flower garden. She was there to meet Isaiah and her aunt Marsha for dinner, and she was looking forward to the meal, which was sure to be delicious. She always loved going to her aunt's house, since it had been her own for a while and it still felt like a second home to her.

Just before she knocked on the front door, she heard a car pull into the driveway behind her. She turned and saw that it was Isaiah's truck, and she grinned and decided to wait for him.

After he'd parked, he hopped out of his truck, his eyes glued to his phone. He hadn't seemed to notice her waiting there for him, and he was swiping his thumb across his phone screen as if he was texting someone. Across his face was a big goofy smile, and her heart skipped a beat, wondering excitedly what it meant. Her mind immediately began to whirl with optimistic suspicions.

"Isaiah!" she called, and he looked up and smiled at her.

"Hey, sis! What's up?"

"Mm, I think you'd better answer that question first. Who are you texting?"

He froze for a second, his mouth popping open. He slid his phone into his back pocket and she crowed in triumph.

"It's Gwen, isn't it?" She grinned impishly at him as he finished his walk across the front lawn and stopped on the front porch beside her. "You're texting Gwen."

The tips of his ears were decidedly pink as he cleared his throat. "I might be texting Gwen."

"You are!" she crowed. "And you like her! Look at the way you're blushing."

He grimaced playfully and groaned. "Fine. Yes. I do. So much. And I'm texting her."

"I love this!" She clapped her hands, tickled by how bashful he was acting. It was clear that he was completely smitten with Gwen. "You should ask her out."

He scratched the back of his neck. "I—um—"

"Oh, come on, Isaiah! Ask her out. If she's not up for starting a relationship again yet, she can tell you that and you can wait until she is ready. Then at least she'll know you're interested and maybe she'll feel ready for a relationship that much sooner, knowing that you're interested in her."

He cleared his throat. "I can't ask her out."

"Isaiah! Come on," she wheedled.

"I can't because I already did ask her out." A grin spread across his face. "Actually, we're dating."

Olivia's jaw dropped, and then she squealed and thumped her brother's back enthusiastically. "Isaiah! Congratulations! I can't believe you're dating someone!"

He laughed. "Don't sound so surprised, it's not very flattering."

She laughed too. "Oh, you know what I mean."

At that moment, their aunt Marsha opened the front door.

"What's all the excitement about?" she asked.

"Isaiah has a girlfriend!" Olivia squealed, and he blushed.

"You do?" Marsha asked, gasping. "Is it Gwen?"

He nodded, and Marsha and Olivia exchanged a knowing smile. Olivia felt thrilled, knowing her aunt had been hoping this very thing would happen just as much as she had been.

"Oh my goodness," Marsha said, pressing a hand to her chest excitedly. "Come on inside, both of you, so you can tell me all about it."

"I also need the full update," Olivia said, stepping inside the familiar, cozy house. "I just found out a few seconds ago. I demand every detail, Isaiah."

He laughed. "Oh boy, I should have seen this coming. But I'm perfectly happy to talk about it."

They sat down together in the living room, where Marsha had set out some crackers with cheese spread and a pitcher of lemonade. She poured a glass for each of them as Isaiah started his story.

Olivia listened, enraptured, as her brother told them all about realizing that he was developing feelings for Gwen and working up the courage to ask her out. She sipped the delicious lemonade, trying to repress a grin. She felt over the moon that Isaiah had found someone he was interested in, and she had a hunch that the practical, kind-hearted Gwen would prove to be an ideal match for him.

"I like her a lot," he said finally, smiling that goofy smile again as he finished talking about his first date with Gwen. "She's smart and funny and... well, we just seem to get along together really well. It's surprising, I guess, considering how different we are, but we seem to balance each other out nicely."

"Opposites attract," Marsha said, shrugging wisely. "She brings out parts of you that have gotten buried beneath the surface, and you do the same for her. Everyone is complicated and multi-faceted, and sometimes we need someone to come along to remind us who we are. Well, more like who we're capable of being."

He grinned at her. "I like that. That makes a lot of sense. I don't feel like I'm changing for her, I feel like she's drawing new parts of me to the surface."

"What happens when you're done with your work on the school?" Olivia asked, unable to hold the question in any longer. She was squirming with curiosity. "Are you planning on dating Gwen long-distance, or..."

"Well," he said, drawing out the world playfully. "Even before I asked her out, I was toying with the idea of sticking around here. I really like this town. It's got pretty much everything a person needs to be really happy with their environment: a good community, things to do, not to mention access to the ocean." He laughed. "I've been debating staying here in Blueberry Bay longer, and I'm very much leaning toward staying here now, as long as things continue to go great with me and Gwen."

"Ah, amazing!" Olivia clapped her hands, grinning from ear to ear. "I'm so excited about the prospect of you sticking around."

"I am too. And I'm so excited that you've found a woman you like so much," Marsha said, her eyes shining. "This is a wonderful turn of events."

"Now we just have to wait for Mom and Dad to move out here too," he joked. "Then the whole family will be together."

"They might!" Olivia gasped, thrilled by the idea. "They've always talked about moving after they retire, and why not move to this beautiful town where both their beautiful children are? I think it'll be a no-brainer."

"Oh, do you really think they might?" Marsha asked, her hand on her heart. "I absolutely love that idea. We could be like one big happy family again."

"I really do," Olivia said, taking a bite of a cracker. "They've both mentioned how much they like Blueberry Bay, and they keep talking about when they get to visit again. I think it's got an excellent chance of happening."

"I hope so," Marsha said, looking overjoyed.

The three of them continued to talk for a few minutes longer. They spoke excitedly about the future as they sipped their lemonade and nibbled crackers with cheese. Soon a buzzer went off in the kitchen, and Marsha announced that the chicken pot pies were done.

They continued to talk as they sat around the kitchen table together, eating the delicious meal. Olivia's heart felt full, and she couldn't wait to hear about what happened next between Isaiah and Gwen.

CHAPTER TWENTY-TWO

Caitlin moved her fingers dexterously back and forth as she stitched up the edge of Pearl's butterfly costume for Kids' Fest. She pressed her lips together in concentration, focusing completely on her task. She knew that the butterfly costume was important to her daughter, and she wanted it to look wonderful.

It was just one week until her wedding, but for the time being, she was putting all of her wedding-related tasks to the side. It felt refreshing to work on something else for a change—as excited as she was to marry Michael, all of the work of planning the wedding had felt overwhelming at times.

She knew how excited Pearl was for Kids' Fest, and when she'd learned that her daughter's presentation was going to be on butterflies, Caitlin had had the idea to sew Pearl a butterfly costume to present in. Caitlin liked to sew, and it wasn't a difficult project, but after a couple hours of work, her fingers were starting to ache a little.

She leaned back and yawned for a moment, surveying her progress. She saw that she was almost done, and she smiled. She was looking forward to seeing the look on Pearl's face when she got to try on her costume.

"Hey, sweetheart!"

She turned and saw Michael walking through the doorway behind her, grinning at her.

"Hey!" She tilted her face up and he kissed her. "How are you, sweetheart?"

"I'm good. What's all this?" he asked, gesturing to the beautiful black and orange costume on Caitlin's lap. The orange fabric shimmered in the sunlight pouring in through the window.

"A costume for Pearl," Caitlin said. "I'm almost done sewing it, and then I've just got to shape the wire that's inside it."

"I'll help you," he said.

"Would you? I want to sew these little black sequins along the edges here. You want to start on some of those?"

"Absolutely. Hand me that black thread?"

For a few minutes, they worked in companionable silence, and then she caught him looking at her with a sweet smile on his face.

"What?" she prompted, laughing a little.

"This," he said. "You. You're such a good mom to be doing this. A lot of brides wouldn't be able to focus on anything besides their wedding the week before."

She cleared her throat, feeling touched by his words.

"I care about our wedding very much, and I'm so glad we decided to do a bigger wedding instead of a courthouse wedding, but at the end of the day, the thing that matters most to me is my family. In the long run, I care more about Pearl having this costume for her presentation than I do about all the details of our wedding being perfect. Because even if there are some small snafus on the day we get married, it won't really matter, because at the end of the day I'll be married to you. That's enough. That's all that really matters, so I don't need to stress about the small stuff."

He gazed at her, a grin cutting across his handsome face as adoration glinted in his eyes.

"This stuff," she said, gesturing to the craft supplies lying around her, and to his hands as he stitched along the edge of the costume. "This is what I'm really looking forward to. Every day, for the rest of my life. Us having a life together, and all of the little moments that come with that."

He swallowed, and there seemed to be something gleaming in his eyes.

"What?" she asked, tucking her hair behind her ear and suddenly feeling a little self-conscious, he was staring at her so hard.

"I just fell more in love with you," he said, and then laughed breathlessly.

"Oh, sweetheart!" Her heart felt a rush of happiness. It made her love him even more, knowing that he valued her words so much. It meant that he was looking forward to those parts of their marriage as well. "I love you so much."

"I can't wait to marry you," he said, squeezing her hand. "I can't wait for all those little moments."

He leaned forward and kissed her again, and she knew she couldn't wait to marry him either.

* * *

Gwen walked down the hallway of Little Clams Elementary School, feeling a thrill of pride. Her muscles ached with tiredness, and there were speckles of colorful paint all up her arms, but her heart felt full.

It was the day before the big Kids' Fest event at the school, and she and Isaiah had been there together all day, making finishing touches on all of the renovations to ensure that everything was perfect.

At the moment, she wasn't sure where he was, but she was taking one last walk through the elementary school, looking at all of the rooms they'd renovated. It was partly to make sure there weren't any tasks that they'd missed, but it was mainly because she wanted to take a look at all of their hard work and enjoy how good it looked. Each of the classrooms they'd worked on had been transformed from something functional into something spectacular.

She stepped inside one classroom that she was particularly proud of. That room they had painted with all kinds of colors—red, blue, yellow, green, orange, and purple. Each of the walls was painted with thick stripes of the various colors, and the plan was for teachers to be able to use the stripes as a teaching tool. Olivia had come up with all kinds of ideas for how to use the stripes for learning activities, such as organizing words into categories or arranging events onto a timeline. Gwen smiled at how beautiful the walls looked—the room was like a garden of colors. It didn't feel like too much, at least not for a children's classroom—the variety added a sense of energy and excitement to the room that she knew would make the kids eager to learn.

In addition to the colorful walls, that room had some of the new furniture that Isaiah had built, along with one of the new reading nooks. Isaiah had built small lofts in some of the classrooms—structures that were essentially indoor treehouses—and they'd filled them with pillows and crates of books. Those were one of her favorite new additions to the school, and she knew the kids would be absolutely thrilled about them.

She paused by the window, which offered her a fantastic view of the new playground that Isaiah had built. It looked fantastic—colorful and fun, with plenty of structures that would encourage the kids to get exercise while playing games with their friends.

She stood there looking at it for a while, thinking about the man she was starting to date and feeling a surge of admiration for him. When she finally turned around, she jumped a little. Isaiah was standing in the doorway to the classroom, smiling at her. She wasn't sure how long he'd been there, but he had a look in his eyes like he'd been staring at something.

"What are you looking at?" she asked, smiling at him. "The room looks great, doesn't it?"

"The room does look great," he said, smiling and coming toward her. "But I was looking at you."

"Oh," she said, feeling herself flush a little. She didn't know what to say in response.

"You're so beautiful," he said. "Not only intelligent, but beautiful. I'm so lucky I get to date you."

"Beautiful, huh?" she asked, smiling up at him. "Not too inflexible and difficult to be around?"

He leaned forward and kissed her. "Not at all. I like even the most stubborn parts of you."

She laughed, feeling butterflies of happiness flap around in her chest. As they stepped away from the kiss, she noticed a large brown paper bag in his left hand.

"What's that?" she asked, realizing that an incredible savory smell was coming out of the bag.

"I went ahead and got us some dinner from The Crab," he said, grinning at her. "I figured we've earned it, with how hard we've worked today."

"That sounds incredible," she said. "I'm starving."

They laid a blanket down on the floor of the room and set their food out on it. They ate the food hungrily, and she felt that food hadn't tasted that good to her in a long time.

"Thanks for that," she said, when they finished eating. She let out a long, contented sigh. "I owe you one."

"Are you kidding?" he said, lying down on the blanket and looking at the ceiling, grinning. "I owe you. You've done all this work. It's incredible."

As she glanced down at him, she suddenly got an idea. Outside, the sun was setting, and they'd turned the lights on in the classroom so that it wouldn't be too dark. She got up and scampered over to the light switch, turning it off. Over their heads, a miniature galaxy of glow-in-the-dark stars glowed against a navy-painted ceiling.

"Oh, that's nice," he said, grinning at her as she came back and flopped down on the blanket beside him. "We really did a nice job with those stars."

"We sure did," she said, looking up and feeling a pleasant sense of peace wash over her. "It feels so good to accomplish something like this. It was fun, but there's so much satisfaction in knowing that it's all done."

As soon as the words left her mouth, a thought

struck her. She glanced over at Isaiah, suddenly feeling sad.

"What's going to happen now?" she asked softly.

"What do you mean?" he asked, turning toward her with a smile that disappeared as soon as he saw her serious expression.

"I mean," she said slowly, "now that you're all done with the school, what happens with us? Aren't you going to go back home?"

"I've been thinking about that," he said, rolling onto his side so he could look into her eyes without turning his head. "And I'm thinking that I'd like to stay here in Blueberry Bay."

"You would?" she asked, her heart beating faster.

"Not just because of our relationship," he said. "I don't want you to feel that kind of pressure. I really love this town, and I've got family here. But I would be lying if I told you that our relationship wasn't a major part of why I want to stay. I really want to see where things go with us."

She didn't know what to say. Her heart was thumping in her chest, and she felt filled with a mixture of relief, peace, and excitement. The news that he was wanting to stay made her heart feel like it was doing cartwheels.

"Is that okay?" he asked softly, seeming to misinterpret her silence.

She beamed at him, making sure he could see on her face how truly excited she was.

"It's more than okay. That makes me so happy, Isaiah. Really, truly happy. I want to see where our relationship goes too."

For a moment, they smiled at each other, and then he moved his head toward hers. He kissed her, and a lightness like she'd never known before filled her heart.

CHAPTER TWENTY-THREE

Isaiah leaned against the side of the Little Clams' gymnasium with his hands in his pockets and grinned. Around him was a huge crowd of parents and grandparents and kids, all taking part in the Kids' Fest activities. Since he'd worked on the renovations for the school, he'd been invited to the event, and he'd been having the time of his life getting to see how excited the kids were for all of the new additions to their school.

He'd wandered the halls for a while, visiting all of the remodeled classrooms and enjoying seeing the kids' reactions. He'd also spent some time out by the new playground, and all of his pals had come running up to tell him how much they loved it. His heart felt full—not just with the satisfaction of a job well done, but with the happiness that came from helping other people.

Eventually he'd found himself in the gym, which was where most of the activities and presentations were being held. There were arts and crafts tables in one corner, games in another—and at that moment a bunch of kids in costumes were lining up for a costume contest. He noticed Pearl Lewis wearing an incredible butterfly costume and he waved at her.

The whole school was buzzing with noise and energy, and it made him feel great, knowing that he'd been a part of making it all possible. He knew that everyone wasn't just excited about Kids' Fest, they were also excited about the renovations—the little school had been transformed into a better place thanks to all the work that he and Olivia and Gwen had put into it.

He noticed Corey Easton and his kids, Max and Haley, standing by the arts and crafts tables and he grinned and made his way over to them.

"Hey, guys," he said, giving Max and Haley each a high-five. He and Corey exchanged a friendly smile. "How are you all liking Kids' Fest so far?"

"It's awesome," Max said, putting his hands in his pockets as if he wanted to imitate Isaiah.

"I've been making all kinds of art projects," Haley said, her eyes shining.

"Really?" Isaiah said, grinning at her. "Will you show me?"

Eagerly, the eight-year-old showed him the painted rocks she'd been working on, and he was genuinely impressed.

"Those are awesome, Haley," he said, meaning it sincerely. "Hey, speaking of painting—what do you guys think about this mural that Gwen and I painted on the gym wall? Does it meet with your approval?"

"You made this?" Haley asked, looking up in awe at the colorful painting of the planets surrounded by stars and spaceships. "I love it! There are so many beautiful colors."

"Why thank you." He grinned at her. "Neither Gwen nor I consider ourselves to be artists, but we used math to trace the outlines of everything based on a mural template I got. See, you guys, math is useful."

Haley grimaced over the mention of math, but Max grinned up at the mural in admiration.

"It looks great," he said approvingly. "I love the spaceships."

"Did you paint all the classrooms too?" Haley asked.

Isaiah nodded, crossing his arms. "Yes, we did. Do you like them?"

"They look so nice! I especially love that room with all the stripes." Haley lifted her chin in approval, and Isaiah grinned.

"Well, I'm glad we have the thumbs up from an authority on spaceships and from an artist," he said. "I'll have to tell Gwen the good news when I see her."

The kids laughed, and Max bowed. He seemed to like being called an authority on spaceships.

"Hey, everyone!" Olivia stepped up to their group, grinning from ear to ear. She had some paint on her hands, making it clear that she'd also been partaking in the crafts earlier in the day.

"Olivia!" the twins cried, and practically tackled her in a hug. Once she'd embraced them, she stepped up to Corey and gave him a kiss.

"Isn't it all amazing?" she said, her eyes shining. "Isaiah really knocked it out of the park." She turned to her brother and gave him a big hug. "I can't even begin to thank you enough for all of the work you did. The school has never looked better. You're amazing."

"Aww, shucks," he said, grinning and feeling a warm feeling in his stomach. "It was a lot of fun."

"Good. It's been so fun having you here in town." She rested her hands on her hips. "The fact that you're going to be staying makes me so happy I could burst."

"I'm pretty happy about it too," he said honestly.

The five of them continued to talk together—Olivia and Corey had all kinds of ideas for how Isaiah should spend his summer, and they agreed that Corey and Olivia and Gwen and Isaiah should go on a double date together soon. The twins interjected opinions here and there—Haley told Isaiah that he should take Gwen for a long walk along the beach to look at the starfish, and Max said that they should go to an amusement park and play with the bumper cars.

Finally, Corey suggested that they go outside and play some of the games. Isaiah's interest perked up at the suggestion—he knew that Gwen had volunteered to take over the slip-and-slide booth later in the afternoon, and he wondered if she was there yet.

The five of them made their way along the hallways of the school until they reached the green lawn in the back of the building. There the school had set up a variety of games and activities—a bouncy house, pony rides, potato sack races, and a slip-and-slide.

Sure enough, Gwen was manning the slip-and-slide booth, looking more relaxed than ever. His heart lifted when he saw her laughing with some of the kids who were stepping up to the booth. She was wearing a t-shirt and a baseball cap, and she looked like someone on vacation and having a wonderful time.

As he watched her, he knew that he was meant to stay there in Blueberry Bay. Although Gwen wasn't the only reason he was planning to stay in town, he felt like she was the reason why fate brought him there. He felt as though he had been destined to meet her.

All I knew was that I felt antsy with my old life in North Carolina, he thought, unable to keep from smiling. *But it was like I knew in my gut that I needed to leave—because my future was here.*

At that moment, Gwen caught sight of him and raised her hand in greeting. Grinning, he started toward her, excited to spend the rest of the event by her side.

* * *

Gwen covered her mouth with both hands, laughing over the antics of one of the kids, who was going down the slip-and-slide for what must have been the seventeenth time. Beside her, Isaiah laughed loudly, also delighted by the kid, who seemed to be a natural-born comedian.

"Be careful!" Gwen called out, although the kid wasn't doing anything dangerous at the moment. Her overly-cautious reflexes made her want to speak up just in case, but after she'd said the words she reminded herself that the kid had been being careful, and she could trust him to look out for himself and the other kids.

She hadn't expected to enjoy manning the slip-and-slide booth so much, but she'd been having a wonderful time. Now that Isaiah was there with her, she was having even more fun. The kids were all enthusiastic and adorable, and she was enjoying being out in the sunshine. She'd always been good with people—especially kids—but this felt different from working as a doctor. She was able to be more relaxed and let her hair down a little, and she was finding it pleasant to work with kids in a no-pressure setting.

When it was time for the next volunteer to take over the slip-and-slide booth, she and Isaiah wandered around the school and grounds together, looking at all of the hard work they'd accomplished and enjoying watching the kids playing games. They stopped to talk to a variety of people they knew, and she was introduced to all kinds of people that she'd never met before.

It's good to get to know more people of Blueberry Bay, she thought, smiling to herself as she and Isaiah stepped away from a conversation with a couple that she'd never met before. *And it's nice to meet them here when we're all having fun.*

After another hour or so of wandering and taking part in some of the activities, Kids' Fest started to wind down. Kids and parents began to wander back to their cars, calling goodbyes and chatting happily about their prizes.

"How are you feeling?" Isaiah asked, wrapping an arm around her.

"Tired." She laughed. "But feeling so accomplished."

"You should be," he said, giving her a squeeze. "The place looks amazing. Everyone was so excited about the new renovations."

"Good." She heaved a contented sigh, leaning into his embrace. "These are some really great kids. I'm glad we were able to make their school a better one."

They joined the team of people who had

volunteered to clean up the school and grounds after the event. The work didn't take long with so many hands working, and as they were finishing, Corey invited Isaiah and Gwen to come get dinner with him and Olivia and his kids.

"We thought we should celebrate how well everything went," Corey said, clapping Isaiah on the shoulder. "Not only today, but also the fact that all of the renovations got finished on time."

"You were still worried, weren't you?" Isaiah said to Olivia, crossing his arms at her in a teasing manner. "You were worried we weren't going to get everything done in time."

"I was." Olivia laughed, swatting his arm. "And you have to admit, without Gwen's help, we wouldn't have gotten it all done by today!"

"We would have," he protested. "I just wouldn't have slept."

Everyone laughed, and he turned to Gwen with a grin. "But Olivia is right. We couldn't have done it without you, Gwen. We're so grateful."

"Oh, shucks," she said, laughing, and Olivia hurried forward to give her a hug.

"I'm so glad you came here," she whispered, and Gwen's heart lifted up. She was glad she'd come there too.

The six of them went out to dinner at The Crab, which was crowded but able to squeeze them in at a table in the back.

"I'm so excited about eating," Max announced. "It's already been four hours since I had that hot dog."

Gwen chuckled, feeling her own stomach grumble. She and Isaiah had nibbled on snacks at Kids' Fest, but she was more than ready for a full meal.

The restaurant around them was filled with conversation and laughter, and their own table was fun and rowdy because of all the energy that Max and Haley still had even after their long day. Max kept them all entertained with a slew of terrible jokes, and Isaiah threw a few of his own into the mix. They laughed and groaned good-naturedly as they ate their meal.

"Hey, everyone!"

Sandy and Daniel Ryan stopped by their table on their way to the door. With them was a smiling teenager that Gwen had never met, and an adorable baby boy.

"Kids' Fest was amazing, wasn't it?" Sandy asked.

"Yes, it was!" Haley agreed enthusiastically. "I've never made so much art in one day before."

For a while, Sandy and Daniel chatted with their table, discussing how much fun the day had been. After a while, they went on their way, and in another moment Alissa and Dane Taylor waved to their table as they entered the restaurant. Gwen was struck by how close-knit the town was, and how pleasant that felt.

She looked around, holding Isaiah's hand under the table. The restaurant was filled with people that she'd seen that day at the school, and she recognized some of her patients as well. She realized in that moment what her life could really be like in Blueberry Bay—she could be truly part of a community.

And that's what I want, she realized, feeling her heart lift up. *That's exactly what I want.*

She felt surprised that it had taken her so long to recognize it—maybe because she'd never been a part of a community like that before.

Isaiah squeezed her hand under the table, and she turned toward him with a smile.

"What are you thinking?" he asked playfully.

She met his gaze, squeezing his hand back. "I'm just thinking that it's really nice to be home."

CHAPTER TWENTY-FOUR

Alissa grinned to herself as she sat in bed, looking at her phone screen. It was a beautiful sunny morning, and she'd just woken up. The first thing she'd done was text her twin sister Caitlin.

ALISSA: Good morning! How are you feeling?

Caitlin had replied immediately.

CAITLIN: Like I'm made of glass.

ALISSA: Hmm. Like in a good way or a bad way?

CAITLIN: Good way. Like I'm made of glass and I'm full of sunlight. But also nervous.

ALISSA: Sounds like a totally normal

way to feel on the most important day of your life!

It was the day of Caitlin and Michael's wedding, and Alissa felt tingly with excitement. She could hear Dane singing quietly to himself as he washed his face in the bathroom, and she knew he was also looking forward to the wedding.

CAITLIN: You're right. I can't wait for my twin hug. That will help settle my nerves.

Alissa's heart warmed. She felt so happy for her sister, knowing she was about to have the loving marriage she deserved. She could relate to Caitlin's wedding jitters, since her own wedding was still fresh in her mind, and she smiled to herself, remembering how good and exciting it had all felt.

ALISSA: Perfect. And you get a bonus Oscar hug along with the twin hug.

CAITLIN: Yay!

Chuckling, Alissa climbed out of bed. She felt as light as a feather emotionally, despite the fact that being so far along in her pregnancy made her a bit cumbersomely heavy physically.

"Good morning, beautiful," Dane said, stepping out of the bathroom and grinning at her. "How are you feeling?"

"So excited." She grinned back at him. "I'm going to be counting the minutes until the ceremony starts."

After eating a healthy breakfast, they worked together around the house for a while. She kept glancing at the clock, and he teased her about how impatient she was being. Finally, after lunch, they got ready for the wedding together—he zipped up the back of her beautiful light blue dress for her, and she helped him straighten his tie.

She took a deep breath as she sat down to put on her flats—she was feeling a little winded. Oscar was due to be born in about a week and a half, and her body seemed to be feeling the effects of pregnancy more than usual.

"You okay, sweetheart?" he asked, hurrying to her side. "Are you in pain?"

"No, no pain." She smiled up at him, grateful for how attentive he was being. "Just feeling a little winded."

"Let me put your other shoe on," he said, kneeling down and putting on her second flat.

"Wow, I feel like Cinderella," she said, laughing.

"Well, you *are* my princess."

That made her grin, and as he finished placing

her shoe on her foot, her heart swelled with love for him.

"You look so beautiful," he said softly. "Just as beautiful as on our wedding day. I'm going to be thinking a lot about our wedding today, I just know it."

"I am too." She took both of his hands in hers. "I'm so happy I married you, honey."

"Right back at you. Married life has been amazing. I feel like I love you even more now than I did when we got married."

She leaned down to kiss him. "I feel that way too. You've been such a rock for me during this whole baby adventure."

"Strap in, it's about to get more exciting."

She laughed, and he grinned at her. He stood up and then helped her to her feet, chuckling as she checked the time yet again.

"Hey! It's actually time to leave now," she cried, feeling ecstatic. "Are you ready?"

He laughed. "Yes, I am."

She couldn't have contained her smile if she had tried. "Then let's go watch my sister marry the love of her life."

They got into the car and drove down to the beach, to the spot where Michael and Caitlin's wedding had been set up. Rows and rows of white chairs lined the beach, facing the ocean and a white archway that had been adorned with colorful flowers. Her heart hammered with excitement as she got out of the car and looked around for her twin.

"I bet she's in that tent there," Dane said, pointing to a white tent placed a stone's throw behind the chairs. "You know—hiding so Michael doesn't see her yet." He chuckled.

She grinned at him. "I bet you're right. You go ahead and sit down, sweetheart. I'll meet you there in a little bit—first I want to give her a hug."

He nodded, smiling, and started to make his way down to the front of the seats. She turned in the direction of the tent, unable to keep from grinning. She felt giddy with happiness for her sister, and she couldn't wait to see her in her wedding dress.

"Knock knock!" she called at the entrance to the tent. "Is there a bride in here?"

The front flap of the tent was instantly pulled back by Pearl, who looked adorable in a pink frilly flower girl dress.

"Yes, there is!" Pearl announced joyfully.

"Alissa!" Caitlin called from inside the tent. "Come on in."

Alissa stepped inside the tent, and her eyes

immediately locked onto her sister. Caitlin was wearing a beautiful dress with a long, silky skirt, and her hair had been done up elegantly, with pearls and small flowers tucked into the up-do.

"You look gorgeous!" Alissa cried and hurried forward to give her sister a hug.

Caitlin squeezed her back tightly, and Alissa could feel that the bride-to-be was shaking a little bit.

"Feeling nervous still?" she asked sympathetically as they pulled away from the hug.

Caitlin shook her head, smiling. "No, I'm just so happy. I feel like I'm dreaming or something."

"You want me to pinch you?"

"No!" Caitlin laughed. "I'll realize it all soon enough. I think once Michael's actually standing there in front of me, I won't feel like I'm dreaming anymore."

For a moment, the sisters stood there grinning at each other, and then Alissa pulled her twin into another hug.

"Caitlin?" someone called from outside the tent. "Everyone's here. It's almost time."

"Oh my goodness," Caitlin said, and Alissa squeezed her hands, grinning.

"Take a deep breath. I love you! I'll see you out there."

"I love you too. See you out there," Caitlin said, her eyes shining.

Alissa took one more look at her twin, feeling her heart swell with happiness. Then she hurried out of the tent to take her place next to Dane. She couldn't wait to watch her sister walk down the aisle.

* * *

Caitlin watched Alissa slip out of the tent, feeling a surge of excitement and happiness.

"Good luck, Mommy!" Pearl said, running to give her mother a hug.

"You too! Have fun being the flower girl," Caitlin said, hugging her daughter back tightly.

The wedding coordinator came to get Pearl, and Caitlin felt her heart pounding with excitement. She turned to look at herself in the mirror that had been placed inside the tent. She really did look beautiful, she thought, and unexpectedly, tears filled her eyes. She felt like the luckiest woman in the world, getting to marry Michael—and in such a beautiful setting, surrounded by so many people who loved both of them.

"Caitlin?" The wedding coordinator stepped inside the tent. "It's time."

Caitlin followed her outside the tent, blinking in the sunlight. It was a perfect day—a clear blue sky arched overhead, and the sunlight was warm and golden. A light breeze from the ocean kept the temperature the perfect degree.

Her eyes traced over the white chairs where all of their friends and family members were sitting, and she smiled, seeing so many people that she knew and loved. She saw many of them turn around and smile at her, all of them looking happy and excited.

Past all of the guests, standing in front of the white archway covered in flowers, was Michael. She couldn't quite see his face from that distance, but she seemed to be able to sense the shining look that was in his eyes. She took a deep breath, feeling as though she couldn't wait to get down the aisle and reach his side.

Her father stepped up to her, giving her a big hug.

"Are you ready?" he whispered, and she nodded.

The music began, and Pearl went down the aisle first, tossing flower petals gracefully. Caitlin's heart gave a little squeeze of happiness as she watched her. She felt proud of the calm, measured way in which Pearl performed her part of the ceremony.

The music changed, and Caitlin's dad gave her

arm a squeeze. Together they began to walk down the aisle, and everyone stood. She heard murmurs all around her, but she was hardly conscious of anything except Michael. He was staring at her with tears welling in his eyes, looking like the happiest man in the world.

Her dad kissed her head at the end of the aisle, and then she took her place beside Michael. Her soon-to-be husband took her hands in his, and she squeezed his tightly, feeling that he was her anchor to the world. As she'd predicted, it all suddenly felt real instead of like a dream, and her heart raced as love filled her chest.

The officiant smiled at both of them, and then gave a short speech about the challenges and rewards of marriage. Caitlin did her best to listen, but her head was spinning a little. She was gazing into Michael's eyes, feeling as though she could get lost in him.

Michael began to speak his vows, which he'd written for her, in a calm, steady voice. "Caitlin, I love you. I vow here to love you for the rest of my life. While I can't control everything in the world, I *can* control my actions, and I promise to support and defend and love you with my actions for the rest of my life. I want all of the little moments of our life together to be valued and treasured just as much as the big moments of passion, like this one. I'm going to love you through the daily struggles and the moments of success. I'm going to love you through sickness and health, through richer or poorer, forsaking all others, for as long as we both shall live."

Her heart soared, seeing the love in his eyes as he spoke the words, and she had to blink back tears.

Soon it was her turn to vow to him, and she took a deep breath, ready with all her heart to promise to love him for the rest of her life.

CHAPTER TWENTY-FIVE

Gwen's eyes misted up with tears as she watched Caitlin and Michael say their vows to each other. Even though she didn't know either of them particularly well yet, she felt happy for them. It was clear they loved each other very much, and watching them say their vows to each other warmed her heart.

Isaiah was sitting beside her, smiling his big, sweet smile. He was the one who had been formally invited to the wedding, since Olivia and Caitlin had become good friends since Olivia had moved to Blueberry Bay. Gwen was there as his plus one, and she felt lucky to have been included. It made her feel even more that she was part of the community, seeing something so special and being part of it.

I can feel the love all around me, she thought, feeling herself get a little teary-eyed in a good way. *Not just from Michael and Caitlin for each other, but from everyone sitting here for the two of them.*

Almost as if he could sense her thoughts or her tears, Isaiah reached out and squeezed her hand. She turned toward him, squeezing his hand back and looking into his eyes for a moment. She could feel the connection between the two of them growing, and for a second it made her heart race.

She found herself thinking about her past, and how tense she had been about so many things. She'd once imagined herself marrying Ron—an outcome she was now very grateful had never occurred. She thought dryly to herself that if she'd married Ron, she never would have looked the way Caitlin looked just then—almost beside herself with happiness, eyes shining, and clearly filled with love. If she'd married Ron, she would have been standing there stressed about details and wanting everything to go exactly a certain way. She realized in a flash that her overly-precise nature had come from a desire to fix the way she'd felt with Ron. He had felt wrong, and rather than admit to herself that he was wrong for her, she'd tried to fix all the little details of their lives together instead. She'd been clinging to structure and precision, hoping it would make the way she felt unsatisfied with her life go away.

But it never could have, she thought, feeling her eyes fill with tears again. *Love makes you feel differently than that. Love makes you feel right. Love makes you feel safe.*

All of the things she'd once feared and thought weren't right for her, she'd been wrong about. She did like to take time to rest, and to have fun—and she was more than capable of letting loose sometimes. It wasn't those things that weren't right for her, it was just that her old relationship hadn't been right, and that had made everything else not feel right.

She glanced over at Isaiah, and her heart swelled to see the way he looked at Caitlin and Michael with so much affection. But what about with the right person? With the right person, someone she knew would support her and help her find hope and optimism no matter what? With that person, everything felt easy.

He glanced at her and grinned when he saw her looking at him. He leaned sideways a bit to press his shoulder against hers, and even that small contact between them made warmth flow through her.

Michael and Caitlin finished their vows, their

eyes shining at each other, and then the officiant smiled at them.

"I now pronounce you man and wife—you may kiss the bride!"

Michael took a deep breath, tucking a loose wisp of hair behind Caitlin's ear.

"Come on, Michael, kiss her!" Pearl cried from the front row.

People cheered and laughed, and Michael dipped Caitlin back in a passionate kiss. Gwen felt tears rush to her eyes—she hadn't thought that kind of love happened in real life anymore. But she was starting to believe it was more than possible.

Michael and Caitlin started to walk back down the aisle together, holding hands. Both of them looked exquisitely happy, and a little dazed. People stood up and cheered for them again, clapping and calling out congratulations.

"Well," Isaiah said, turning to Gwen with a grin. "I guess it's time for a party."

Michael and Caitlin stood at the end of the aisle and greeted all of their guests warmly as they passed through. Then they went off with the photographer to take wedding photos, and the guests all pitched in to help with the change-over, moving chairs from the ceremony area over to where the tables for the reception had been set up.

"This is lovely," Gwen said, admiring how beautifully the tables had been decorated, and the strands of lights that had been strung up on poles around the dining area. "It's clear they put a lot of thought into all this."

There was an hour set aside for cocktails and mingling before the reception officially began, and Isaiah and Gwen wandered around talking to the other guests. The sun was starting to dip toward the horizon a little, flushing the sky with pink. A balmy breeze from the ocean offered just the right amount of coolness, although Gwen guessed she would be making a run back to her car to get a sweater before the evening was over.

There was a volleyball net set up along the beach near the reception area, and some guests were playing volleyball there with a beach ball. Isaiah and Gwen went to join Olivia and Corey's team, where they were introduced to Luke Ward and Hannah Jenkins.

"My dad is dating your boyfriend's aunt," Hannah said, explaining the connection to Gwen cheerfully. "Look—there they are over there. Adorable as always."

Gwen laughed, delighted by Hannah's friendly manner and affectionate attitude toward her father and Marsha. The game of beach volleyball was a great deal of fun, although she'd never have expected herself to take off her heels at a wedding and play a game barefoot in the sand.

After the game of volleyball, Isaiah and Gwen got a couple of glasses of Sauvignon Blanc and wandered along the water's edge for a while. As they strolled, taking deep breaths of the fragrantly salty air, they passed Sandy and Daniel Ryan and their baby Chandler and paused to say a quick hello. It was a cheerful conversation, and Gwen felt again that she was lucky to live in a town with such kind people in it.

"It's such a beautiful day," Gwen said as she and Isaiah stepped away from the conversation and continued to walk, her voice soft. She felt thoughtful but energetic at the same time—she was looking forward to the rest of the celebration, but also to going home and getting to sit quietly and think for a while. She felt that she had a lot to process, after seeing so many wonderful things that day.

Isaiah reached down and slipped his fingers through hers.

"It's got me feeling all kinds of sentimental for

sure," he said, looking at her with emotion burning in his eyes.

Her heart rate picked up as she wondered just what his expression meant, but she didn't ask. At that moment, a bell rang, calling everyone back to the reception area for dinner.

The strands of glittering lights had been lit, adding a fairytale-like atmosphere to the dining area. The food was served buffet-style, and Gwen and Isaiah ran into several more people that they knew as they stood in line and got their food. She noticed Alissa and Dane at the front of the line—Alissa's expression was almost as radiant as Caitlin's, she looked so happy.

The food was delicious. There had been a variety of options, and Gwen had chosen mashed potatoes, empanadas, popcorn shrimp, and a side salad. She and Isaiah sat down at a table close to the water's edge, and although the wind was getting a little stronger, it was still warm enough that the effect was pleasant.

They were seated with Josie and Wesley Cliff, as well as with Josie's sister Paige Garner. Gwen noticed the young woman looking slightly nervous, and she wanted to ask her if anything was the matter. She felt it wasn't her place, however, and since Paige still laughed often throughout their table's animated discussions, she decided that whatever was bothering her couldn't be that serious.

The sun sank below the horizon, and the stars came out overhead, shining like diamonds against a tapestry of deep blue. Around them, the night was filled with the sounds of people talking and laughing. She had a good view of Caitlin and Michael sitting together at the head table, and the way they kept looking at each other with shining eyes warmed her heart.

"Look, Paige, this is it!" Josie whispered in a triumphant tone as Michael and Caitlin stood up together.

"Oh no," Paige murmured in a small voice.

"Nonsense," Josie said, leaning over and wrapping an arm around her. "It's going to be incredible and you know it."

"What's going on?" Isaiah asked curiously.

"Paige baked the wedding cake," Wesley said, smiling proudly at his sister-in-law.

"She just graduated from Flourish Baking School in Providence," Josie added. "Top of her class. She's the best baker for miles, and Blueberry Bay is lucky enough to have her wanting to start a bakery here."

"That's awesome," Isaiah said, grinning at the young woman. "I can't wait to taste this cake."

Paige smiled weakly. "Thanks. I'm so nervous it didn't turn out well."

"You strike me as someone who pays attention to details," Gwen said, smiling at her. "As long as you baked the cake carefully, which I'm sure you did, I'm sure it turned out beautifully."

Paige smiled gratefully at her, and then they all turned toward where Michael and Caitlin were about to cut the cake.

"Aren't they adorable?" Josie murmured.

Michael and Caitlin held the knife together and cut the first slice of cake, and everyone cheered as they fed each other bites from it. Michael laughed as Caitlin accidentally smeared a little frosting on the side of his mouth, and then his eyes widened when he tasted the cake. Even from a distance, it was clear to see that he mouthed the word "wow" after swallowing.

"Looks like it's a hit, Paige," Josie said, thumping her sister's back and grinning triumphantly.

"Or he said 'wow' because he thinks it's bad," Paige said nervously.

Her sister laughed and stood up, pulling Paige to her feet.

"Come on," she said. "The cake table is open for guests now. Let's all go try this wedding cake and then we can decide for ourselves."

They took their place in line and were some of the first people there. The catering staff sliced the cake with expert speed and precision, and the line moved quickly. The bottom tier of the cake was chocolate, and the top tier was lemon. Alongside the growing number of slices was a hand painted sign that read, "Baked by Paige Garner. Check out her bakery website!" with a website link written below it.

Gwen eagerly chose a slice of lemon cake, while Isaiah took chocolate. They both took a bite as soon as they'd stepped away from the cake table, not wanting to wait. Gwen was alight with curiosity— she wanted to know if Paige had succeeded as well as Josie was sure she had.

"Whoa," Isaiah said, looking floored.

"Oh my goodness," Gwen said. "This is the best cake I've ever had."

He nodded emphatically. "Paige!" he called to the young baker. "This is amazing!"

Paige laughed and flushed, looking pleased. She was soon surrounded by people congratulating her on the success of her cake. Gwen overheard several people say, "I'm definitely going to check out your website," and a few people asked her about baking for their private events.

Michael went up to Paige and gave her a hug. "Thank you so much, kiddo. We couldn't have asked for a better wedding cake."

"Oh, of course." She smiled, her eyes shining. She looked both thrilled and relieved.

"I'm wondering if you have the time to work for me again this summer," he said, grinning at her.

"Oh, well, I—"

"Not as a barista. As our exclusive bakery supplier. A business partnership with Tidal Wave Coffee. What do you say?"

Paige's jaw dropped, and then she started to grin. "Yes! That would be amazing."

Josie gave her sister a hug, and Gwen couldn't help smiling. She liked the young woman and was glad that she was finding success—it was clear that she deserved it. Gwen had never tasted such a flavorful, mouthwatering cake, and she knew that Paige must have worked very hard to become that good at baking.

Isaiah and Gwen stood to the side of the reception area, continuing to stand as they enjoyed their cake. When it was announced that people could go up for seconds, they both got a second slice of cake, both of them trying the kind they hadn't chosen the first time. Gwen found the chocolate cake to be every bit as delicious as the lemon cake.

"Ladies and gentlemen, it's time the first dance," a teenage D.J. wearing a bowtie announced into a microphone. "Michael and Caitlin O'Neil, please take your places on the dance floor."

"Oh," Gwen cooed, placing her hand on her heart. "I love first dances."

Isaiah turned to her with a sweet smile, and then both their attention were caught by the sight of Michael and Caitlin stepping onto the dance floor together, holding hands. The dance floor was a makeshift one made of wood and placed under the strands of lights. Gwen thought the scene looked marvelously picturesque, with the moonlit ocean sparkling behind the newly-wedded couple.

A sweet love song began to play over the speakers, and Michael took Caitlin in his arms. Slowly, the two of them began to waltz across the dance floor. It was an imperfect waltz—Michael stumbled a few times, which made his bride laugh. Gwen felt tears spring into her eyes as she watched them—she'd never seen a couple look so much in love before.

Suddenly, she heard someone gasp nearby. She

looked over and saw Alissa clinging to her husband's arm and staring down at the sand below her. It was damp underneath her legs.

"What happened?" Isaiah asked, looking around in confusion.

Gwen, quick to realize what was happening, answered his question. "Alissa's water just broke. She's about to have her baby."

CHAPTER TWENTY-SIX

Dane turned to his wife, wondering what had happened. He'd never heard Alissa gasp like that before—clearly something was wrong.

She held tightly to his arm, her eyes wide.

"What is it?" he asked.

"My—my water broke," she whispered.

His jaw dropped and his mind began to race. Instantly he went into protector mode, determined to take care of her and make sure that everything worked out just fine. In the back of his mind, he felt a surge of excitement that he was about to meet his son, but he remained focused on what he needed to do.

"Okay," he said. "We're getting you to the hospital."

His wife blinked, still holding tightly to his arm. She seemed a little stunned—he knew she hadn't been expecting this to happen at all—neither of them had been.

By then, enough people had realized what was happening, and murmurs of surprise and concern were rippling through the guests. There was enough of a hubbub that Michael and Caitlin noticed, and they stopped dancing. The second Caitlin looked at her sister, she seemed to know what was happening, and she hurried over to her side.

"It's time?" Caitlin asked, taking Alissa's hands.

"I guess so," Alissa said breathlessly. "But don't stop your dance! I hate to interrupt your wedding like this."

"Nonsense!" Caitlin said. "This is so much more important than our wedding."

"But maybe I can just push through to the end of the wedding," Alissa said. "I hate to miss it—"

Dane shook his head firmly, and around him, their friends and family members were urging her to go to the hospital right away.

"Alissa," Johanna said firmly, taking her daughter-in-law by the arm. "You need to leave now."

Alissa took a deep breath, looking apologetically

at her twin sister. "I'm sorry—this is the worse timing. I feel so bad for interrupting your reception."

Caitlin shook her head. "Don't you feel bad for an instant," she said, squeezing her sister's hand. "It's a baby—they're always on their own schedule, and this little guy decided to come early."

"I think he wants to be a part of the wedding," Everett joked, and Johanna swatted his arm good-naturedly.

"Sorry, buddy," Dane said to Alissa's stomach. "We won't get back in time for that."

"Shouldn't we just stop the wedding?" Caitlin asked. "I always told myself I'd go with you to the hospital, Alissa."

"Absolutely not." Alissa squeezed Caitlin's hands. "I will absolutely not allow you to leave your wedding reception. You stay here and finish your evening as planned. I will be just fine."

"But—"

Alissa shook her head. "Keep celebrating."

"I'll call you regularly with updates from the hospital. How's that?" Dane asked, smiling at his sister-in-law. "I promise."

Caitlin hesitated for a moment, biting her lip, and then she nodded. "All right. You'd better hurry—the hospital is pretty far from here."

Since there wasn't a hospital in Blueberry Bay, the townsfolk always went one town over for baby deliveries. It wasn't terribly far, but Dane felt his stomach slosh with nervousness when he thought of the distance.

"I agree. Come on, let's get going," he said, wrapping an arm around his wife.

"Okay," Alissa said weakly.

He began to usher her toward their car, eager to get her to the hospital. Around them, people called out well-wishes and encouragements, and he and Alissa smiled at them as best they could while still moving at a hurried pace.

Michael and Caitlin and Johanna and Everett and Alissa's parents followed them to the car. Alissa insisted that they all stay at the wedding, and they reluctantly agreed. The group waved to them as they drove off, calling out encouragements.

"We're so lucky to have a community like this," Alissa murmured as Dane took the turn out of the parking lot as quickly as he could carefully do. "I feel so loved right now."

He glanced over, resting a hand on her knee. "You should. You are."

"Such bad timing, though, Oscar!" she cried, patting her stomach and pretending to reprimand their baby. "I wanted to finish watching my sister's first dance."

"We can watch the recording later on," he assured her, and she nodded, smiling at him.

"You're right. Thanks, sweetheart. And honestly, I'm so excited to meet Oscar that it does feel worth it."

"What an eventful evening, huh?" he said, chuckling. "If I'd known this was going to happen, I would have worn more comfortable shoes."

"Tennis shoes and a suit jacket and tie," she said, laughing. "That would have raised a few eyebrows."

He drove them carefully to the hospital, and it wasn't until they arrived that he realized he'd been white-knuckling the steering wheel.

"I'll drop you off at the door," he said. "That way you can check in right away. Do you need me to come in with you?"

"No, I'm okay," she said, smiling at him bravely. "Thanks."

She squeezed his hand and then stepped out of the car. He watched her take a few steps forward gingerly, and he winced a little, able to see that she was in pain.

As soon as he'd parked the car, he jumped out of it and ran into the hospital. Alissa had just reached the front desk, and he hurried to her side. She turned to him, laughing a little.

"You ran in here?"

He nodded, and he caught the receptionist hiding a smile.

The hospital staff was kind and communicative, and it wasn't long before Alissa was settled in a delivery room. A nurse came by and announced that Alissa was going to give birth very soon, and that she would come back with the doctor in a matter of minutes.

"Just stay comfortable and keep taking deep breaths," the nurse said. "It won't be long at all."

She slipped out of the waiting room, and Dane turned to his wife with a brave smile. "How are you feeling, champ?" he asked, squeezing her hand.

She squeezed his back tightly. "Um..." She took a deep breath. "I have to admit, now that the moment is here, I feel really overwhelmed. I—I'm not sure I'm ready."

He leaned forward and looked her in the eyes. "Alissa Taylor," he said. "You absolutely are ready. You've been ready for a long time. I know it all feels like a lot right now, but that doesn't mean you're not ready. You can do this. You're going to be an amazing mom."

She smiled at him warmly, and he thought he caught a glimmer of tears in her eyes. "Thank you."

"Of course. I have to admit, I'm nervous myself about becoming a father—"

"You're going to be an amazing dad!"

"Thanks, sweetheart. It's a lot for us both to take on, but I know we can do it. We're going to do it together and support each other. We're going to have each other's backs. I'm so grateful you're my wife, and that we get to start this next adventure together."

He stood up and bent over her, giving her a kiss. She smiled up at him, and she seemed to be feeling less nervous than she had been.

"You ready, Oscar?" he asked, patting her stomach. "You be a good boy now. Don't give your mommy a lot of trouble."

Alissa laughed, and then winced as she felt another contraction. "I can't wait to meet him," she said, grinning at her husband.

At that moment, the nurse and the doctor stepped inside the room, and Dane squeezed his wife's hand, feeling a rush of adrenaline. They were going to meet their son very soon.

CHAPTER TWENTY-SEVEN

Caitlin gazed into Michael's eyes as they danced together under the stars. She felt more full of positive emotions than she ever had before in her life. She'd just married the man of her dreams, and her sister was about to have a baby.

"It's been quite the day, huh?" Michael asked, grinning at her.

He seemed to be practically glowing with happiness, and just like her, he couldn't seem to stop smiling. He hadn't wanted to stop dancing with her. They'd barely left the dance floor since their first dance as husband and wife, and she wasn't complaining.

She loved dancing with him, and their dance floor area was exceptionally beautiful. Twinkle lights glowed overhead and danced in a fragrant breeze from the ocean, and in the distance, over the sound of the music, they could hear the soothing sound of the surf rushing up against the sand. The stars winked and sparkled overhead, and she couldn't help feeling that their wedding had been the most perfect event of her life.

"Quite the day." She let out a soft sigh. "I feel thrilled that I'm married to you, and thrilled that I'm about to become an aunt. I couldn't think of two more exciting things to be happening at once."

He nodded, his eyes warm and soft. "A lot of new beginnings," he murmured, and then leaned in for a kiss.

The evening seemed to pass in a whirlwind. She and Michael continued to dance, and she loved looking around at the smiling faces of all their guests. Everyone seemed to be having a great time, and most of their friends and family members were out on the dance floor with them.

The night had been filled with laughter and love, and she felt incredibly blessed to be surrounded by people that she cared for so much. Pearl was dancing with a group of other children, looking like a little fairy princess in her pink dress. Caitlin's heart warmed to see her. She looked so happy, and she overheard her tell several people that she was about to have a cousin and that she was extremely excited.

She saw Isaiah dancing with Gwen, the new doctor, and she had to hide a grin. She loved the idea of them as a couple, and they looked adorable together.

She saw Corey dancing with Olivia, their heads held close together, and Johanna and Everett swing-dancing like a couple of teenagers. Hannah and Luke were standing on the side of the dance floor, eating cake and laughing hysterically about something. Marsha and Willis were walking along the beach together, holding hands and talking happily. Sandy and Daniel were sitting near the dance floor, showing off Chandler to Josie and Wesley, who looked absolutely captivated with him. Just in front of them, Paige and Tommy were dancing, and their dance moves seemed to include some kind of secret handshake.

Many of the guests came up to congratulate her and Michael and wish them well. Most of them asked if they'd heard anything from Alissa or Dane, and she kept having to shake her head and say, "Not yet."

She exchanged a few sympathetic glances with Johanna as they waited. Although she was having a wonderful time, she felt impatient for news from her sister, and she kept checking her phone, which she kept inside a pocket that she'd had specially made for her wedding dress.

"Nothing yet?" Michael asked as she slipped her phone back into her pocket for what must have been the fifteenth time.

"No." She smiled at him but couldn't help sighing. "I feel all pins and needles." She laughed. "I just want to know what's going on."

He nodded and kissed her head. "It might be hours before the baby arrives. I'm sure everything is going just fine."

"I know," she whispered. "You're right. I should focus on our celebration. I'll hear from them as soon as the baby is born, I'm sure."

They stepped away from the dance floor for a while to talk to more of their guests and enjoy second slices of cake. After another hour or so, things began to wind down and guests began to depart slowly.

"One last dance?" Michael asked, taking her hand and steering her toward the dance floor.

"Yes—and let's ask Pearl to join us."

Grinning, Michael called for Pearl, and she came running up to them and took their hands. For a moment, they were the only three people on the dance floor, dancing along to an upbeat song. Soon other people joined them, seeming to sense it was the last song of the night.

The final chords of the song sounded, and everyone cheered and started to hug each other. As the group hug began to break apart, Caitlin heard her phone ding in her pocket.

Her heart leapt up and she reached inside her pocket eagerly. She sucked in her breath when she saw that it was a text from Dane.

DANE: He's here! Oscar has been born. Both he and Alissa are doing great.

"I'm an aunt!" Caitlin exclaimed, and everyone cheered again.

"Yay!" Pearl shouted and grabbed Michael's hands. The two of them began to dance around together, whooping with excitement.

"We should go to the hospital," Michael said, panting and grinning.

"Could we?" Caitlin perked up eagerly. "I would love that."

"I want to go as well," Johanna said, and Everett echoed the sentiment.

A group of them—including Caitlin's parents, Everett and Johanna, Marsha and Willis, and Josie, Wesley, and Paige—decided to leave the reception to go see the baby. The remaining guests volunteered to help the wedding decorators clean up, and they urged Michael and Caitlin to leave right away to go meet Oscar.

"It's your wedding day, you're not allowed to do any clean-up." Olivia laughed, seeming to sense Caitlin's hesitation. "We've got it covered. Don't we, Isaiah?"

"We absolutely do," Isaiah said, looking up and grinning from where he was starting to fold up chairs next to Gwen. "You go meet your little nephew. And then spam Olivia with pictures so she can send them to me."

"All right," Caitlin said, laughing. "Thank you all so much."

"Of course," Sandy said, waving her away. "Go meet Oscar!"

The group that was going to the hospital hurried along the beach to the parking lot, where they piled into their cars, laughing and bantering with a sense of eagerness. Caitlin was tingling with excitement as they started their drive, and behind her in the back seat, Pearl was starting to sing a little bit, as if she couldn't express her feelings any other way.

Beside Caitlin, Michael reached over and took her hand.

"You're my wife," he whispered.

Happiness rushed through her, so sweet and full she thought she might burst.

"Forever and always," she said, and at the next stoplight, he leaned in for a kiss.

* * *

Alissa gazed down at Oscar, feeling aglow with feelings of love and joy. She couldn't quite believe he was really hers yet—but there he was, with big brown eyes and a tiny little nose and the smallest fingers.

"Are you real?" she whispered to him, stroking the side of his cheek.

Beside her in the delivery room, Dane grinned. His eyes were shining, and he looked a little dazed, but Alissa knew he was the proudest father in the world.

She felt exhausted—she hadn't been in labor for a terribly long time, but it had still been an incredibly taxing experience. But it had been more than worth it—gazing down at her little boy, she felt she'd never had such a sense of wonder and delight.

"I just can't get over how cute he is," Dane said, staring at Oscar with a kind of awe. "I've never loved anyone or anything this much this fast before. I mean, I loved him before he was born, but now..."

His words trailed off, and he smiled.

She beamed back at him. She didn't need him to finish his sentence, she knew just what he meant.

She gazed down at Oscar for a few more moments, imagining getting to bring him home and putting him in his crib. She imagined her parents and Johanna coming over, and Caitlin too.

"Oh!" she said, turning to Dane hurriedly as that thought sparked another in her brain. "Did you let everyone know that he's been born?"

He nodded, smiling. "I let everyone know almost right away. Caitlin didn't text me back, but I have a feeling that means she's speeding over here with Michael."

She laughed, feeling a glow of excitement at the thought of her twin sister getting to meet her baby. "How long do you think it will take for people to get here?"

"Less than five minutes," he joked. "Or maybe they'll just teleport here from the wedding, and we'll see them in a couple of seconds."

She started to laugh, and then she cocked her head to one side as she heard voices in the hallway outside. It was soon clear that they were voices she recognized.

"It seems your prediction of a couple of seconds was correct," she said, starting to laugh again. "I think that's them arriving now."

She and Dane grinned at each other, and in the next moment, their friends and family members burst into the delivery room.

Alissa felt tears rush into her eyes as she saw their smiling faces. Caitlin hurried forward and gave her a gentle sideways hug, being careful not to bump Oscar.

"Oh, he's just gorgeous," her twin breathed. "Sorry you missed the reception, buddy," she said to the baby, waving at him with a huge smile on her face.

"Don't worry, there will be plenty more weddings in Blueberry Bay," said Johanna, her eyes dancing, and she and Alissa shared a grin.

"Come on in, have a seat everyone," Dane said, looking like a proud father with his eyes shining. "There's not quite enough chairs for everyone, but we can make do."

Their guests spread out around the room, some of them taking chairs but most of them seeming to be too excited to sit down. Everyone stared at Oscar in adoration, proclaiming him to be a beautiful baby.

"What's his name?" Paige asked, looking a little starstruck as she gazed at him.

"Oscar," Alissa answered. "It took Dane and me an extremely long time to think of it, but we finally both came up with 'Oscar' at the same time, and we love it."

"I do too," Caitlin said, nodding. "It suits him."

"I love it too," Josie declared. "It's cute and dignified at the same time."

Everyone else agreed that Oscar was a great name. Alissa gazed at all their faces, feeling aglow with love. Marsha was blinking back tears of happiness, holding onto Willis's arm, and Johanna looked like the proudest grandmother in the world.

"We're so excited for you both," Wesley said warmly. "Congratulations. We know you're going to be amazing parents."

"So lovely to meet you, Oscar," Caitlin said softly.

Alissa's heart filled with gratitude as she looked around at their friends and family members. She and Dane and Oscar were surrounded by people who loved them and were going to support them—and back in Blueberry Bay, they had even more friends who would do the same.

He's going to be so loved, she thought, feeling tears spring to her eyes.

She reached out and took Dane's hand, knowing that their little one was going to have an amazing life, growing up in Blueberry Bay.

Thank you so much for reading the *Chasing Tides* series! If you're curious about Whale Harbor—the town right next Blueberry Bay—and want to find out more about it, I have another series set there!
Start with *Whale Harbor Dreams*.

ALSO BY FIONA BAKER

The Marigold Island Series

The Beachside Inn

Beachside Beginnings

Beachside Promises

Beachside Secrets

Beachside Memories

Beachside Weddings

Beachside Holidays

Beachside Treasures

The Sea Breeze Cove Series

The House by the Shore

A Season of Second Chances

A Secret in the Tides

The Promise of Forever

A Haven in the Cove

The Blessing of Tomorrow

A Memory of Moonlight

The Snowy Pine Ridge Series

The Christmas Lodge

Sweet Christmas Wish

Second Chance Christmas

Christmas at the Guest House

A Cozy Christmas Escape

The Christmas Reunion

The Saltwater Sunsets Series

Whale Harbor Dreams

Whale Harbor Sisters

Whale Harbor Reunions

Whale Harbor Horizons

Whale Harbor Vows

Whale Harbor Blooms

Whale Harbor Adventures

Whale Harbor Blessings

**The Chasing Tides Series
(set in Blueberry Bay)**

A Whisper in the Bay

A Secret in the Bay

A Journey in the Bay

A Promise in the Bay

A Moonbeam in the Bay

A Lullaby in the Bay

A Wedding in the Bay

A Future in the Bay

For a full list of my books and series, visit my website at www.fionabakerauthor.com!

ABOUT THE AUTHOR

Fiona writes sweet, feel-good contemporary women's fiction and family sagas with a bit of romance.

She hopes her characters will start to feel like old friends as you follow them on their journeys of love, family, friendship, and new beginnings. Her heartwarming storylines and charming small-town beach settings are a particular favorite of readers.

When she's not writing, she loves eating good meals with friends, trying out new recipes, and finding the perfect glass of wine to pair them with. She lives on the East Coast with her husband and their two trouble-making dogs.

Follow her on her website, Facebook, or Bookbub.

Sign up to receive her newsletter, where you'll get free books, exclusive bonus content, and info on her new releases and sales!

Made in the USA
Columbia, SC
01 November 2024

45446441R00193